WATERLOO SUNSET

Recent Titles by Judith Saxton

THE BLUE AND DISTANT HILLS
HARVEST MOON
THE PRIDE SISTERS
SOMEONE SPECIAL
STILL WATERS
YOU ARE MY SUNSHINE

WATERLOO SUNSET

Judith Saxton

SEVERN SH HOUSE

This title first published in Great Britain 1998 by
SEVERN HOUSE PUBLISHERS LTD of
9–15 High Street, Sutton, Surrey SM1 1DF.
Originally published 1980 under the title
Follow the Drum and pseudonym *Judy Turner*.
This title first published in the U.S.A. 1998 by
SEVERN HOUSE PUBLISHERS INC of
595 Madison Avenue, New York, N.Y. 10022.

British Library Cataloguing in Publication Data

Saxton, Judith, 1936-
  Waterloo sunset
  1. Napoleonic Wars, 1800-1825 - Fiction
  2. Love stories
  I. Title II. Turner, Judy, 1936-. Follow the drum

823.9'14 [F]

ISBN 0 7278 5373 2

Printed and bound in Great Britain by
MPG Books Ltd, Bodmin, Cornwall.

For Dennis and Audrey Owens, with love.

Acknowledgements

My especial thanks go to Mrs Winifred Parry
of Wrexham for the help and advice she gave
me over the French which has been used where
appropriate, and to the staff of the Wrexham
Branch Library, who obtained for me such an
abundance of memoirs and journals written by
the soldiers who fought at Waterloo.

CHAPTER ONE

It was cold in the garden, for though it was May, with darkness an almost wintry chill had fallen. But on the terrace outside the ballroom at Ulverstone Grange, two small figures, silhouetted against the lights, watched the dancers circling beneath the crystal chandeliers, and almost forgot their numbed fingers and toes.

"Can you see Master Harry, Miss Babs?" The taller of the two young women said presently. "I don't reckon he's come, for he's so tall and 'andsome we'd have noticed him first off."

Barbara sighed, shaking her head. "No, Becky, he hasn't come, and I don't suppose he will, now. When we met in the shrubbery to say goodbye, two days ago, he said he'd be off to join his regiment the following day unless orders were changed. But he's only at Harwich and I did think he might get back, just for Elmira's ball."

"If he'd come back and found you not dancing, I 'spect he'd have made a great botheration," Becky said. "It's not right, Miss, your aunt not letting you go to the party. It's because you're so much prettier than Miss Elmira, and because they're jealous that you've fixed Mr. Harry's interest, whilst Miss Elmira's not got so much as a sniff of a beau!"

"Well, she never liked the Kimberley boys when we were children, and dislikes them still," Barbara said, trying to be fair. "I was always a tomboy, and enjoyed boys' games more than sewing, or playing the piano." She chuckled reminiscently. "And I never had any pride to lose, so I didn't mind always being a fielder at cricket, or being tied to the stake for hours on end when they played at Indians, or being soaked to the skin when Harry's bridge across the stream broke, with me upon it! Anyway, Elmira says Harry's just trifling with me, she's said so time and again. But she'll change her mind when he comes of age and returns home to ask if he may marry me!"

"Oh, Miss, isn't it romantic?" Becky breathed, clasping her hands. "Mr. Harry, off to fight the French and knock old Boney out, just so's he can marry you!"

"Well, not *just* so he can marry me," Barbara said. "I say, Becky, I'm freezing cold! I think perhaps we'd better return to the schoolroom."

Becky, sensibly clad in a woollen dress with a thick shawl round her shoulders, looked with some concern at her young mistress's thin and faded Indian muslin, with its short sleeves and skimpy, high-waisted skirt.

"No wonder you're cold, Miss Babs! But you don't want to go in yet. You wait here and I'll creep in by the side door and fetch your old blue cloak. How would that be?"

"Oh yes, lovely. But do hurry," Barbara begged,

rubbing her arms briskly. "I'm sure if I don't get warm soon I'll be found here by Perkins in the morning, frozen to a pillar of ice!"

"Like Lot's wife," Becky said, inaccurately but fervently. "That would make milady think twice about making you miss the party!"

"Yes, but it wouldn't be much consolation to me," Barbara pointed out. "Do hurry, Becky!"

Becky trotted off, leaving Barbara to press her nose against the window and wonder when the next dance would begin. Even as she watched she saw her uncle, Lord Landrake, signal to the orchestra to stop playing. She saw him speak, though she could hardly make out the words, then realised he must be announcing supper, for a discreet evacuation began, led by Elmira and her mama.

Barbara watched until her cousin, straw-coloured hair piled high, disappeared from view, and then stood back to consider. Should she go back to the schoolroom after all? Plainly, Harry Kimberley would not arrive now to gladden her heart with a glimpse of his Grecian profile, his curly fair hair, his laughing blue eyes. And the dancing was finished, for a while at any rate. On the other hand, it was fascinating to see the girls in their filmy, light-coloured gowns and the young married women in their more dashing confections. Just listening to the faint strains of the music was enough to set one's feet tapping. It would be dull in the schoolroom, with only Becky for company.

She was still hesitating when, with a protesting squeal of hinges, one of the long windows was flung open, letting a gust of warm air billow out into the night. Someone stepped through the opening on to the paving, and a deep, masculine voice said, "Don't trouble to come with me, David; you go and get yourself some supper. All I want is a breath of fresh air and I'll be right as ninepence, you'll see."

Barbara had flattened herself against the wall and she remained still as stone whilst the man closed the long window carefully behind him. He turned and walked a few paces, muttering, "Phew! Wish I could blow a cloud! But at least it's quiet out here. I'd rather face cannon than have my ear battered by my hostess all evening!"

He crossed the terrace, stumbling a little, and Barbara heard him curse softly beneath his breath. Then he leaned on the parapet, looking down into the quiet garden below. Barbara took a deep breath and expelled it soundlessly. She was safe enough now, but when the stranger turned to go back into the ballroom he would be bound to see her. She must act at once. If she tiptoed quietly across the terrace she could gain the steps which led down on to the lawn. Once there, it would be a simple matter to run across the garden and re-enter the house by the side door.

To think was to act, and she stole softly towards the steps. Only let her gain them and she would be away in a second! Her slippers were soft as moth's wings, whispering across the paving. She was behind him, almost past. . . .

And then a hand reached out and caught her by the arm.

Long participation in the games of the Kimberley brothers was all that stopped her from crying out. As it was she gasped, before saying resolutely in her small, gruff voice, "Pray don't clutch me so tight, sir! I've no designs on your purse!"

The grasp on her arm tightened. "What are you doing then, skulking out here in the dark?" She felt herself swung round until she was facing into the shaft of light from the windows. "Good God, a girl! I thought you were a lad!" The voice softened a little. "A pretty girl, too. What on earth are you doing here? Why aren't you dancing? Don't pretend you've been in the ballroom, because I wouldn't have missed a pocket Venus like you amidst that parcel of dowdies!"

Barbara stiffened. "*A pocket Venus*? You think me a dab of a female, then? Well, I am not, even if I appear small beside my cousin. How *dare* you!"

"Your cousin? Is she in there? Come, lass, who are you?"

"I'm Barbara Campion, Elmira Landrake's cousin," Barbara admitted. "Lord Landrake is my guardian. Who are you? It's unfair of you, sir, to hold my arm so tight and keep me facing the windows, so that I can't catch a glimpse of you!"

Her captor laughed and obligingly moved so that his own features were illumined, revealing a high-bridged nose, a wing of dark hair flopping over dark eyes narrowed against the light, and a firm mouth with lines running from nose to chin, giving him an appearance of sternness which made Barbara more eager than ever to escape from his grasp.

She subjected him to a swift, close scrutiny, then said, "Well? Who are you? I'm sure I've never set eyes on you before!"

His hand slid down her arm and he caught her fingers lightly, bowing. "Captain Daniel Alleyn, at your service, Cinderella. Will you not return to the ballroom with me? I'll be bound you waltz like thistledown, for you made no more noise than a shadow, running across the terrace."

"I couldn't possibly. My aunt expressly forbade me to attend the party. But I daresay it's a dull affair, after all."

Despite herself, a trace of wistfulness crept into her voice, but the Captain said bracingly, "Sadly flat, to be sure, until I came out for a breath of fresh air and caught a most enchanting little nymph out on the terrace! Well, if you won't return to the ballroom with me, we'll dance out here."

"We shall not! It wouldn't be at all the thing," Barbara said, a suspicion creeping into her mind that Captain Alleyn might have drunk too deeply of Lord Landrake's champagne. Why else should he want to dance on the terrace with a sixteen-year-old in a shabby dress, when in the ballroom young and fashionable ladies waited eagerly for partners?

Inside the orchestra had struck up a waltz, and the strains came lilting across to them. Captain Alleyn bowed again, still with her hand imprisoned in his. "May I have the pleasure of this dance, Cinderella?"

"I must go in," Barbara said distractedly. "Please let me go, I'm so cold!"

He did not seem to attend to her words, for he took

her firmly into his arms, holding her so close that she was warmed by his nearness. And then they were waltzing, swirling, turning, moving as gracefully and surely as though they had waltzed together a thousand times, instead of being strangers.

Barbara had practised the waltz many times with Elmira or Becky, but now she was lifted into enchantment. When he suddenly drew her to a halt she felt as an angel must feel when it tumbles from heaven; she was cold again, the music lacked enchantment, the paving stones were hard once more beneath her thin satin slippers.

"Midnight's struck, Cinderella," Captain Alleyn said softly. "The guests have begun to desert the supper room and presently they'll begin to come on to the terrace. Off with you, unless you want to be caught."

She moved obediently towards the steps and just as she was about to descend them, he caught her shoulder.

"Oh! Goodnight, Captain Alleyn," Barbara said, hoping he would not prevent her from leaving before other guests began to drift into the garden.

He grinned down at her, his teeth gleaming in the faint light. "Goodnight, sweetheart," he said. Then he bent and kissed her.

It was a light enough kiss, but without at all meaning to, she moved a little nearer to him and felt his arms harden round her and his mouth possess her own more firmly. A rush of sudden warmth and pleasure, frightening her with its intensity, made her pull back, fighting to be free of his embrace as suddenly as she had melted into it moments earlier.

He took no notice, holding her closer yet, his mouth seeking hers once more, his breathing quickening. Barbara, heart hammering, her body still traitorously enjoying his closeness even as panic rose and bade her free herself, kicked.

The satin slipper could not have hurt him but it brought him back out of whatever madness had made him sweep her into his arms. He stood back, looking down at her, his expression rueful, even a little guilty. "Never been kissed before, Cinders? Well, I've remedied that, at any rate! Now off with you, before the wicked stepmother comes on to the terrace."

"I . . . I think you must be drunk, Captain Alleyn, to take me for a village slut who will kiss any man who asks! You're detestable!"

He nodded. "Alas, you're right. But you must be detestable too, Cinders, for you enjoyed it, you know you did! So pretty you look when you're indignant, with your eyes bright as fire and your cheeks flushed! I've a good mind to do it again!"

Barbara could hear the stir and murmur as people crossed the ballroom towards the terrace. Being a truthful girl, she did not attempt to defend herself, merely saying hotly, "No gentleman would behave so! I hate you, and I hope I never see you again!"

He took a step towards her and she hastily descended on to the lawn, prudence advising her to retreat rather than risk his making good his threat in front of half Lord Landrake's guests.

He made no attempt to follow her, but as she fumbled with the side door she glanced back and saw him still standing on the terrace, watching her.

"You'll see me again, Cinders," he called, his deep voice carrying easily across the lawn which separated them. "Will you accept my apologies for the kiss? It was, perhaps, a little early in our relationship. When next we meet, propriety shall be my watch-word!"

She did not answer, but slipped inside the house and closed the door, then stood against it for a moment, her heart hammering.

When she was calm, she went along the corridor and up the short flight of stairs to the schoolroom where she found Becky, like a lion at bay, desperately chattering to the housekeeper, Mrs. Garland. At her entry, Mrs. Garland turned round, beaming.

"Milady said to bring you a tray of food, Miss Barbara," she said, indicating a laden tray which stood on a small table near the fire. "I fetched it myself, to mek sure you had some of all the dainties, for I know how you love your food! A real shame, to my way of thinking, that you're not down there now, dancing the soles out of your slippers. But there, when you're a bit older, perhaps."

Barbara thanked the housekeeper wholeheartedly and after chatting for a little about the various guests, the older woman left and Barbara and Becky settled down to eat the elegant repast she had brought them.

"I couldn't get away, Miss, not without letting on that you was in the garden," Becky said. "Lor', but I felt bad! Poor Miss Babs will be frozen, I kept thinking. An' then I thought, she'll be in presently, to see what's 'appened to me. My, I was that glad to see you!"

As she climbed into bed that night, Barbara wondered why she had not told Becky of her encounter with Captain Alleyn. After all, it had been quite a little adventure for one so repressed as herself. Then, remembering the kiss, she thought perhaps it was as well she had not spoken of it. Even remembering his embrace was like fire running along her veins, but she told herself that it was shame and disgust which she felt. He had treated her like a loose woman; if she had responded by behaving like one, as he had seemed to imply, she could only put it down to her youth. In fact if she had behaved badly, it was *his* fault, for he was a soldier, an experienced man of the world, whereas she was not yet out and still, therefore, scarcely more than a child.

Resolutely, Barbara wrenched her thoughts away from the dissolute Captain Alleyn. How differently she would have felt, she told herself, had it been Harry who had kissed her so ardently, Harry whose arms had warmly enclosed her! She remembered that when he had bidden her farewell he *had* kissed her – a soft, reverent brushing of their two young mouths as different from Captain Alleyn's passionate kiss as cool spring water is different from heady wine.

Hastily, she wished the comparison undone; that was not what she had meant at all. Captain Alleyn had been drunk, had taken advantage of her inexperience, and had frightened her half to death into the bargain. By the time she eventually fell asleep she was half convinced that she had been mauled by a drunken brute and was lucky to have escaped with her virtue still intact.

Yet her dreams were certainly not of Harry Kimberley, and a smile curved her lips as she slumbered.

CHAPTER
TWO

"WELL, Babs, I had a great success at my ball! My card was filled and several gentlemen wanted more than one dance, I can tell you. I was much admired, and received innumerable compliments."

Elmira, a heavily built but handsome blonde with a hard face and pale eyes, gave an artificial titter of laughter and glanced contemptuously round the schoolroom, where Barbara was sitting, mending a rent in her shabby brown riding-habit. "So now I shall wait for Papa to have gentlemen visitors, and for invitations!" she concluded.

"I'm glad," Barbara said. "Which gentleman was most attentive, Elmira?"

Elmira considered, absently smoothing the fur trim round her new olive-green pelisse. "Well, Lord Rugeley's son seemed very impressed. And of course Bettina Scowe's elder brother, not that I care for *him*. Otherwise, there was . . ."

She was interrupted by Becky, banging hastily into the room.

"Oh, beg pardon, Miss Elmira, but your Mama says she's ready to set out, and would you please go down now. And to tell you there's a *man* closeted with your Papa! A very fine gentleman, Miss!"

Elmira was all attention, the colour in her cheeks darkening. "A young gentleman, Becky? Did you see him? What's his name?"

"I saw him go into his lordship's study," Becky said. "He's not young, but he seemed *very* distinguished. He walks with a cane, and has silver hair, and a good figure. He was wearing a lovely coat, Miss!"

Elmira got to her feet, buttoning her pelisse and straightening her bonnet. "How exciting! A caller, and so soon! There were several very distinguished older gentlemen present last night, of course . . ." She waved a careless hand to Barbara. "But there, time will tell. I shall see you later, cousin. And who knows what news I shall have for you by then?"

"Isn't she foolish?" Barbara sighed as soon as her cousin had disappeared. "As if anyone would make anyone else an offer on the strength of one meeting! Why, Harry and I have known one another for ever, and it is only recently that he has begun to talk of marriage!"

Despite Elmira's words, it was late afternoon before she again appeared in the schoolroom and then she was obviously out of temper, sitting down on a chair with a thump and complaining crossly that the fire had been recklessly made up with complete disregard for who must pay for the coals.

"I've had a tiresome drive with Mama," she volunteered after a moment. "Dear me, my head quite aches with hearing praise of my looks and my dress."

20

She hesitated, but Barbara, trying somewhat inexpertly to fashion a velvet hairband out of a thin, patched piece of material, merely continued her work. "You know the gentleman caller, Babs? Well, you'll think this quite absurd, but it was *you* he wanted to see Papa about!"

Barbara's work fell into her lap. Unbidden, a picture of a tall, dark-haired soldier with hard hands and demanding lips entered her mind, but she only said with as much calm as she could muster, "Me? Why me?"

"At first I thought it must be a mistake because you're not even out, let alone eligible. Oh, I don't mean you're not perfectly respectable, for you are, but you've no dowry. Still, you've caught someone's eye!"

She tried to speak lightly but her chagrin was evident, though Barbara noticed nothing.

"Have I? Whose? And what did he want with my uncle?"

"He asked Papa's permission to pay his addresses," Elmira said sulkily. "He's the Earl of Chacewater and a widower, I know that much."

The slender tower of hopes which Barbara had been building fell with a crash. "Well, I've never heard of the Earl of Chacewater, and I certainly shan't marry him," she said firmly. "I'm promised to Harry; I don't want to marry an old widower!"

"*Just* what I told Papa!" Elmira said triumphantly. " 'She won't want to marry him,' I said. 'He's too old for Babs'." She lowered her lids to hide the gleam in her eyes. "But Papa was adamant.

'She'll do as she's told,' he said. 'It's an excellent match.' He's told the Earl to return tomorrow, when you must give him your answer. Except that Papa says it shall be yes."

"I can't understand it," Barbara said, her face sheet-white. "The Earl of Chacewater? I've never even heard of him, let alone seen him!"

"He was a friend of your father's," Elmira said grudgingly. "He's seen you out riding, and thought you a nice little thing. But he's made the offer from pity, very likely, for Papa told him you'd no dowry and precious little chance of a decent marriage. As for all this talk of Harry, I've told you often enough that Harry's a great flirt, and doesn't intend to marry you! He's amusing himself, that's all."

"But. . . . I tell you Harry *is* serious! He will marry me when he comes of age, and that's only another four months. What am I to do, Elmira? I won't marry this Earl!"

Elmira got to her feet. "Nonsense, Babs, you've no option but to do as Papa bids you," she said spitefully. "He's your guardian, and the only relative who's ever taken the slightest interest in you. If you refuse he'll send you away to earn your own living somewhere, and you'll never see Harry again." She tittered. "Or you could *prove* Harry's desire to marry you! Why not run to him and cast yourself upon his protection? He's not far off, and I daresay, if all you say is true, he'd marry you at once! Or at least persuade his mama to help you until his twenty-first birthday."

"How could I? I've no money, and. . . . Oh, Elmira, do come back! What am I to do?"

But Elmira had gone. She went straight to her own room and got out her purse, heavy with money. Then she sat down by the fire, wondering whether her words had fallen on stony ground. Would Babs run away to Harry? Or would her penniless but infuriatingly pretty cousin be married before herself?

She waited, with rare impatience, until she judged that Barbara would have explored every avenue and found no escape, and then she rang her bell. Becky, breathless from running up the stairs, for she had been in the kitchen discussing the latest development with Mrs. Garland, was astounded to be handed the purse, with instructions to "Take this to Miss Babs and tell her Miss Elmira says be sure to make good use of it."

"Oh, Miss! But what's Miss Babs to spend it on?" Becky enquired.

"Don't be impertinent," Elmira snapped, "Babs will understand, even if you do not. Off with you!"

It seemed that Miss Elmira was right, Becky thought, for her young mistress, sitting forlornly in the schoolroom, grasped the purse eagerly, and clasped it to her bosom as though it was the one escape from all her difficulties.

"Though what Miss Elmira means you to buy with it, I don't know," Becky said, her face rosy with curiosity.

"She means me to buy a ticket on the stage-coach

to Harwich, and so I shall," Barbara said. "For once, Elmira was right! If I throw myself on Harry's protection he won't let me down. He wants to marry me, and he'll either do so out of hand or find me some refuge until he is able to do so."

"Oh Miss, you *can't*," Becky said, appalled. "Travel on the stage by yourself, and go to Mr. Harry's billet, or lodgings, or whatever he has! Why, you'd be caught and brought back in disgrace before you'd gone ten miles! And your reputation ruined if you spent a night away from home, I daresay."

"Yes, so I shall borrow a suit of Russell's clothes," Barbara said, beginning to chuckle. "What a good thing he's away at school, for they won't be missed! Dressed as a lad, I've no doubt I'll get to Harwich safely, for my voice is deep for a girl's, and I'm sure in one of Russell's suits and with my hair cut off, no one will connect me with Miss Barbara Campion!"

"Mr. Harry may not like it," Becky said with unexpected shrewdness. "I don't say he wouldn't laugh and encourage you here at home, same's he's always done, but what's good enough for a feckless lass isn't what a man wants in a wife."

Barbara stared at Becky. "Yes, but Harry must understand that this time it is not a romp, but necessity. Fetch me a suit of Russell's clothes, there's a dear, for I must be gone this very night! As soon as it's dark I shall go down to the stables and persuade Lew to ride with me into town so that I can catch the stage for Harwich first thing in the morning!"

"Here we are, Miss, the outskirts of the town," Lew said. "Will you be all right if I leave you? I'll have to walk both ponies back to Ulverstone, since I don't want to risk being heard wi' the pair of 'em. You know where to go for the coach?"

"Yes," Barbara muttered. "Goodbye, Lew, and thank you. You won't tell?"

"Not if it were ever so," Lew said. "Take care, Miss Babs."

Barbara slid off her pony's back and held up her hand. "I'll take care. Goodbye for now, Lew. When next we meet I shall be Mrs. Harry Kimberley!"

"I'm sure I hope so, Miss." As they shook hands the lad remarked, "I should call you Master Bob now, I suppose! Can you manage the bag, Miss?"

"It's nothing," Barbara said. "Goodbye, Lew."

She stood in the road and watched until the boy and the two ponies were out of sight, then picked up her shabby carpet bag, adjusted Russell's cap on her cropped curls, and set off, into the town.

Despite some initial nervousness, Barbara found her new identity easier – and pleasanter – to maintain than she would have believed possible. She bought her ticket, choosing from economy to sit outside, where she found three sporting young gentlemen, a youth of her own age, and a crate of hens, all making a great deal of noise. Within a few moments of starting, she and the youth were chatting like old acquaintances.

"I'm Freddy Cresswell," the youth said. "Want an apple?"

Barbara introduced herself as Bob Garland and gratefully accepted the apple, for she was hungry already, and for a while they munched in companionable silence.

When the apples were no more than a memory, Freddy turned to his new friend. "I'm going to join the Army at Harwich," he confided. "I'll bet you're going to do the same, eh, Bob?"

Barbara nodded. "In a way. I've a . . . a cousin in the Rifles, and I hope he may use his influence to . . . to get me taken on."

"By Gad, a cousin in the Rifles! Not the Ninety-fifth, by any chance?" And upon Barbara cautiously agreeing that this was so, he clapped her on the shoulder in an access of glee.

"A cousin in the bloody, fighting Ninety-Fifth! Well *done*, bantling! I don't think they take Volunteers into the Rifles, mind, because you need training for a brigade such as that. But with your cousin's influence, who knows? You're too small for a rifleman, though, and too young." He nudged Barbara so hard that she nearly fell off the coach. "Run away, eh? Me too! My father refused to buy me a commission. Eldest son, you see; doesn't want to lose me. As if I'd take foolish risks! But I can't miss this, you know. I want to help put Boney to the rightabout, and we'll do it, sure as I'm here!"

Barbara, quite carried away by this patriotic speech, said gamely, "Too small for a rifleman, perhaps. But I'll work as . . . as a drummer, or a stable lad! I don't mind what I do so long as I'm with the army!"

"Well said," Freddy cried. "We'll volunteer together, as soon as the coach reaches Harwich!"

"Certainly," Barbara agreed, making a mental reservation to part from Freddy as soon as they arrived at the port. "Though it would be best for me to find my cousin first."

"Aye, for to lose an opportunity to be attached to *the* brigade would be madness," her new friend said. "I say, would you mind if I came along with you to see your cousin? I'd be an asset to the brigade, I can promise you that! I'm a bruising rider and can shoot straighter than most. I don't want to boast, but I can get me a brace of pigeons any time and they're devilish difficult shots, I can tell you. Do you shoot?"

Barbara, taken off her guard, muttered, "Yes, no, well . . ." and then hastily pointed out that the coach was about to draw up at an inn where they might get a meal and a drink whilst the horses were changed. Freddy promptly led the way into the coffee room, informing Barbara that he had 'plenty of blunt', and insisted on buying them both generous plates of ham and eggs, and then tankards of beer.

"Don't worry, Bob," he said when Barbara tried to pay her share. "If you'll introduce me to your cousin that will repay me amply. What rank does he hold?"

"He's a subaltern," Barbara said. "He's only recently joined, you see, but I'm sure he'll speedily rise, for he's a marvellous shot and a very good rider, and the uniform suits him so well . . ." She stopped in some confusion, realising belatedly that to enthuse over Harry's handsome looks might be unfortunate, but her companion seemed to notice nothing amiss.

"Aye, and if he can buy promotion, as I suppose he can, he'll soon get his captaincy," Freddy said. "I shall buy myself out of the ranks as soon as my father parts with the ready, which will be when he sees I'm serious. Now we'd best take our seats again or we'll be left behind."

As the coach drew into Harwich, Barbara realised that not only would she be unlikely to rid herself of Freddy, but that such a move would not be wise. The streets were crowded with soldiers in the uniform of every imaginable brigade, from infantry to artillery, as well as with women and children.

"The women and their brats are camp followers," Freddy told her. "They're a rough lot, so you stick close to me. And look out for any fellows in rifle green. Then we can ask your cousin's direction."

They pushed their way through the crowded streets and presently, outside an inn with the fascinating name of the Three Cups, they caught their first glimpse of the dark green uniform with the black facings worn by 'the sweeps', as the riflemen were affectionately known. Barbara, feeling quite desperate, wriggled her way through the crowd and caught the officer by the arm. He was a huge young man and glanced down at her, a smile tugging at his lips.

"Please sir, we're hunting for the Ninety-Fifth," Barbara said without preliminary. "I've a cousin in the brigade, and my friend and I want to volunteer."

The young man looked from Barbara to Freddy, his smile broadening into a grin. "So we're enlisting babes and sucklings now, are we? What's your name, lad? And the name of your cousin?"

"I'm Bob Garland, sir. My cousin's Lieutenant Harry Kimberley."

The man puckered his brow. "Kimberley. Johnny Newcome, is he?"

Barbara looked nonplussed, but Freddy said, "Newly joined, sir? Aye, that's so, isn't it, Bob?"

The young man nodded. "Thought so. He's in my company, I believe. A fair-haired fellow, with a passion for hunting. That the one?"

"Yes, that's Harry," Barbara said eagerly. "Where can we find him, sir?"

"In France."

Two pairs of eyes rounded with dismay. "France?"

"Aye, or rather, Belgium. The majority of the regiment has gone long since. You've not seen many rifle coats in Harwich, I'll be bound?" And when they shook their heads, he added, "That's because only those who've been wounded or had some other good reason for their absence were left behind. I've had some discomfort from shot in my thigh and the captain of my company has been troubled by a festering wound in his kneecap. But we're both discharged now, and able to rejoin our regiment. So if you want to see your cousin, nipper, you'll have to take ship for Ostend."

"Oh! Will . . . Will it cost a great deal?" Barbara asked.

"Cost? Bob, have you run mad? We shall go over on one of the transports, of course," Freddy said briskly. "Can you tell us, sir, where we should go to enlist?"

The officer started to give them instructions, then changed his mind. "I'll walk along to the corner with you and point the place out. And look, young 'un, I doubt they'll take you on; there's plenty like you tagging the army already. But if you're in such a hurry to get to Belgium to find this cousin of yours, I could do with someone to give me a hand on the ship. I've got two horses of my own to take across, for I need a big mount; no use relying upon buying an animal in Belgium. What do you say?"

Barbara agreed delightedly just as they reached the corner and their new friend pointed out the office where volunteers should go. "And when you've done, meet me again in the Three Cups," he instructed them. "I'm Lieutenant George Symonds. Likely I'll only be able to fix you up with a meal and a shakedown in the loft over the stables, for there isn't a spare bed to be had in town, but you won't mind that, I daresay."

Barbara and Freddy thanked him and then the two of them went into the office.

When they emerged, Freddy was a volunteer with a uniform and instructions to join a ship at present lying in harbour. He was excited, a little fearful perhaps, but he parted from Barbara with many good wishes and promises to look out for each other in Ostend.

Then Barbara, hurrying back to Lieutenant Symonds, had a bit of luck. A lad was walking just ahead of her, wearing a new uniform with an infantry jacket, almost colourless with age, on his arm and an ancient shako in one hand.

"I'll give you a crown for that old jacket and the hat," Barbara said abruptly, jerking his arm. The boy, after a startled gape, grinned with quick cunning and offered to throw in some equally faded but respectable trousers, for an additional borde.

"What's a borde?" Barbara said, opening her purse.

"A shillin', covey," the boy said, peering hopefully at the cash.

"Right. Here you are!"

In a moment the money and the clothes had changed hands and Barbara was hurrying into the coffee room at the Three Cups, where Lieutenant Symonds welcomed her with the title of his one and only groom, valet and stableboy, which made her laugh. However, he bought her bread, cheese and ale and then chased her off to the loft, where she curled up in a corner beneath her blanket and drifted off to sleep in the company of more rogues than she had ever rubbed shoulders with in her life. But they were not interested in little lads, nor she in them.

Next morning she was introduced to her new charges, Hannibal, a great bay stallion with feet the size of dinner plates and mild, enquiring eyes, and

Black Celt, black as his name but with a tempera-
ment which many a lamb might have envied.

"They're used to sea travel, which doesn't mean
they like it," the Lieutenant told Barbara. "I'll go
aboard first, with Black Celt, and you follow with
Hannibal. Once they're below, we'll just give 'em a
glance now and then. The wind's in our favour so we
shan't be afloat long. If you'll give me a hand in
getting them ashore, then we can make our way
directly to where the regiment's billeted. Are you
willing to work with the company's horses? There
are several officers who can't afford grooms and
would be glad of your services."

"Oh, certainly," Barbara said recklessly. "I've
always been good with horses, sir, and I want to be
with my cousin."

She was uncertain whether she had made up her
own mind or had it made up for her, but one thing
was sure; she was going through with it. She would
go to Belgium and find Harry, and then he would get
her out of the scrape as he had got her out of so many
in the past. And until then, she would enjoy her new
freedom.

For being a boy was a freedom she had scarcely
imagined. To walk along the streets alone, peering
into shop windows, exchanging badinage with other
lads; to wander into the coffee room of an inn and
buy oneself a drink; even the freedom from petticoats swishing round one's calves – all these things
were marvellous to Barbara, after her dull and repressed existence with the Landrakes.

And now, climbing aboard the good ship *Adven-*

ture, whose very name seemed a good omen, she could not for the life of her conjure up any worries. She was enjoying herself immensely, and best of all, she was going to Harry!

CHAPTER
THREE

"THEY'RE lowering the horses over the side, Bob. As you can see, there's a good deal of confusion on the beach and I don't want to risk losing Hannibal or Celt. So you and I, lad, are going ashore without delay, and then we'll strip off and wade into the sea and bring the horses out. Two of the animals have been drowned already because they strayed further along the coast and the tide race caught them. The bottom's full of holes, too, so be careful when you go into the water. Is that all clear?"

Barbara nodded. "Yes, Mr. Symonds. Shall we go ashore now?"

"We'll leave the ship as soon as we can, but they're nowhere near my mounts, yet. It takes a while to clear the hold. I did wonder whether you'd do better to go overboard with 'em, but I think not. You might get trampled, or just plain drowned. So we'll stick to the plan I've outlined. Come on!"

They had arrived at Ostend to scenes of almost indescribable confusion. At first Barbara had been fascinated by the crowd of onlookers standing along the jetty, the women in their national costume and elegant, tapering straw hats, beribboned and gay

with flowers. But then she had realised that somewhere in the milling throng on the beach Harry
might be waiting, and her interest switched to the
shore.

Now, following Lieutenant Symonds' broad back,
she made a startling discovery. As they trotted up the
beach, men were stripping off their clothing and
leaving it neatly piled on the sand so that they might
go into the sea after their horses. Others, happily,
were only removing their jackets and shoes, but
Barbara feared the Lieutenant would prove to be one
of those hardy souls to whom bathing meant stripping. Suppose he tried to make her strip? Barbara's
cheeks warmed at the thought.

She glanced round her. The beach looked like a
cross between a horse show and a gypsy fairground,
for the camp followers had literally encamped upon
the sands, waiting to see where the regiments would
be sent. Everywhere women sat on bundles, sur-
rounded by children, equipment, and such bits and
pieces of food and property as they had managed to
get aboard the ships. Some of the horses had already
come ashore and were being rubbed down and re-
saddled, and soldiers in various stages of undress
were charging in and out of the waves, shouting
advice, yelling to each other, and generally enjoying
a thoroughly rowdy and companionable time.

Lieutenant Symonds stopped and began to strip
off his tight-fitting jacket and pantaloons with a
complete disregard for onlookers.

"Come, lad, they'll be bringing Hannibal and Celt
up from the hold any moment," he admonished. "I

want to be in the water and pulling them ashore before they've had time to panic."

As slowly as she dared, Barbara removed her shoes and stockings and then, with infinite care, peeled off her jacket. Her fingers had gone hesitatingly to her shirt fastenings when the idea, in all its beauty, struck her.

"Hannibal's over," she shouted, and at the same moment charged down the beach and into the little waves. "Don't worry, sir, I'll be with him before he's had a chance to stray!"

Behind her, she heard the subaltern's muffled exclamation as he pulled his shirt over his head, and then she was surging further forward, the icy cold water up to her waist, and seeing to her total astonishment that she had spoken the truth all unknowingly, and that Hannibal was indeed in the water! The great horse by no means approved of this sudden cold bath either, and neighed shrilly, throwing back his head and rolling his eyes. Barbara, plunging recklessly on, intent on putting the greatest distance possible between herself and the lieutenant's kindly desire to see that she kept her clothing dry, found to her relief that she had almost reached Hannibal; for that sagacious animal, seeing land, had headed straight for it and had not taken the more circuitous route to avoid the men in the water, which behaviour had proved fatal to two of his erstwhile companions.

She reached Hannibal and jumped up to catch at his halter rope, then turned and made her way towards the shore. She passed Lieutenant Symonds, who merely said, "Well done, Bob. Have you a change of breeches?" And without waiting for a reply he continued to splash towards where Black Celt was squealing with alarm as he saw the relentless waves getting nearer and nearer his nice warm stomach.

Barbara, breathless, soaked from the waist down, her hands slipping on the wet rope and her feet constantly having to dodge Hannibal's big hooves, nevertheless felt a sense of achievement and satisfaction. The water was a caress, for as she neared the shore the shallower waves felt warm to her chilled skin. She laughed aloud, looking up to admonish Hannibal, who was delicately blowing against her hair, his silky upper lip twitching as he tickled himself on her curls.

And then, quite near, a voice said, "Get the grey for me, could you, lad? I've had a ball in my knee and the wound mislikes salt water."

She looked up, the laughter still curving her lips, straight into the face of Captain Alleyn.

For a moment, shock held her rigid, and then she felt warm colour flooding her face, her neck, her whole body, in a tide of embarrassment. Daniel Alleyn, here! And actually speaking to *her*, for she could not doubt that it was she who was so addressed.

However, he seemed to have noticed nothing amiss and she realised he was looking, not at her, but at Hannibal.

"Ho, so George has arrived, has he? I'd know that gigantic nag anywhere! Come on, Hannibal, I'll rub you down whilst the nipper goes and gets

Snowcloud." He grinned at Barbara, friendly but nevertheless commanding. "You can't miss her. She's white as . . . as a Snowcloud, I suppose."

He stretched out his hand for the halter and Barbara faced back into the sea once more. But with what relief! Anything which would allow her to regain command of herself, to decide how to behave towards Captain Alleyn, was welcome. She could see Snowcloud, a beautiful white mare with a flowing mane and tail of silver, being lowered into the water at that very moment. As the first waves splashed her hooves she lifted them up, fastidious as a cat, and Barbara could not help laughing at the anxious way in which the mare watched her warm, white body being lowered into the cold, green-blue sea.

And then she stopped laughing, for Snowcloud must have been one of the unlucky ones. The sea-bed was as uneven as the lieutenant had said, and the mare must have landed in a sizeable hole, for she disappeared completely. One moment she was there and the next the cradle snaked up empty, to be fastened round the next animal as though Snowcloud had never been.

Without a second thought Barbara launched into the quick, choppy swimming stroke Harry had taught her years ago, when they had secretly swum in the river on hot days. It brought her speedily over to where the mare, thoroughly terrified, was rising to the surface, choking and gasping, water streaming from every hair, her great dark eyes wild with fear.

"Good girl, good Snowcloud," soothed Barbara. She put her feet down cautiously and discovered a firm stretch of sand. "Come here then, my beauty."

Snowcloud heard the calming note in Barbara's voice and began to swim towards her. As soon as she was within reach, Barbara tugged an apple out of her pocket and held it out, fondling the mare's ears and neck, smoothing back the confidence with every movement until Snowcloud stood firm once more, crunching on the apple, ears pricked.

"There, my beauty," Barbara said. "We'll go ashore now, eh? Come along then." She grasped the halter rope firmly and turned towards the shore. And for the first time, glanced down at herself. Her shirt was soaked, of course, and was adhering lovingly to her small, apple-shaped breasts in a way which no shirt should ever do on a stripling named Bob Garland!

For a moment horror rooted her to the spot. But Snowcloud's muzzle, pushing her in the back, reminded her that there was no escape. She could not remain standing here, up to her waist in water, until her shirt dried! She glanced longingly at the beach. There was her dear, safe little jacket with its faded braid and tarnished buttons. How she wished that it could be spirited to her by some miracle!

But it was no use praying for miracles. Instead she tried to dispose the shirt material away from her body, but it was difficult with her hands ice-cold and Snowcloud nudging her onwards, and with the waves splashing up to threaten her again with exposure. Finally she wrapped her arms across her chest in the attitude of one shivering with cold and hunched up, rubbing her arms.

Further up the beach she could see Lieutenant Symonds rubbing down Black Celt while Hannibal stood looking on. But close to the water's edge that confounded Captain Alleyn still stood, waiting for her.

Barbara took a deep breath. Very well, she would hurry! She began to run through the water, deliberately splashing, so that the few soldiers nearby drew back hurriedly and the urchins who had lined the shallows, trying to catch stray horses in the hope of some reward from their owners, moved out of range.

Captain Alleyn, she was pleased to see, also drew back. He said sharply as she neared him, "Steady, lad, no need to run," but Barbara replied through chattering teeth, "The water's icy, sir. Here's your horse, and I must get my jacket on before I die of cold."

As she splashed past him she thought the Captain gave her an odd look, but she was concentrating grimly on reaching her clothes, and paid him no more attention than she would have afforded any other soldier on that crowded beach. She sank into a huddle beside her clothes, fairly wrenched the jacket on, and did up the buttons with as much relief as though she had really needed its warmth – for in fact she was glowing from the exercise and her own miserable embarrassment.

Before she could make her escape, however, Captain Alleyn was standing before her. His eyes lingered on her face, swept over her now neatly dressed figure, then returned to her countenance. He said, "Better? Though what good a jacket can be over a wet shirt, I can't imagine! But there, you young 'uns are all the same. Hate water, whether it's for bathing or washing in. Yet you swim pretty well, for all that."

"Aye, I've swum since I was a child," Barbara said gruffly. "My shirt'll soon dry out, as will my breeches. And I've dry shoes and stockings."

"That's true." To her horror the captain proceeded to sit down beside her, and taking a pipe from his pocket began, leisurely, to fill it. "I've had a word with George – that is, Lieutenant Symonds. He says you're going to look after the horses in return for your keep and a place at this forthcoming battle. Well, I'm not in favour of picking up stray urchins, but the way you handled Snowcloud makes it plain that you know what you're about, so you may stay. But you must obey my officers, you understand? Even if the orders given are not much to your taste?" He paused whilst she nodded, then added, "George says your name is Bob Garland, but I could swear I've seen you somewhere before. Got any relatives in the regiment?"

"Yes, sir. Harry Kimberley's my cousin," Barbara muttered. For the life of her she could not look him in the eye and speak out!

"Harry? Well, you're not one whit like him, so it's not that. Got any sisters?"

Terrified, Barbara managed to raise her head and answer him with an assumption, at least, of coolness. Now or never, she told herself. If he accepted her story now, she was made. If he called her bluff . . . well, she dared not think of that.

"Not a sister, no, sir. But I've female cousins, and the family look is very strong in us all, I'm told." She hesitated. Would he need more details?

But it seemed she was not to suffer further. "Very likely that's it, then. I can't tell you where I've met your cousins, or even when, but I daresay it was during my recent leave, for I must have met hundreds of young females, I should think."

Barbara was breathing a silent prayer of thanks, pulling on her thick stockings and fastening her clumsy shoes, when he said thoughtfully, "Kimberley. Where have I heard that name recently? I recall thinking it familiar, yet not connecting it with Harry . . ." He brooded for a moment, then stood up. "Well, it seems I'm not destined to remember. You've run away from home, of course?"

"Why, no, sir! Whatever . . ." she wilted under his hardening gaze. In a whisper she amended, "Yes, sir."

"Never lie to me or any other officer, booberkin," Captain Alleyn said, sounding quite friendly now. "I'm not pretending that if I'd met you in England I'd have countenanced this for one moment, but this is Belgium and I've no means of sending you home, nor the slightest doubt that if I did, you'd be on the next packet bound for Belgium with, perhaps, someone less principled than George. But tell me truthfully now, is some poor woman weeping into her pillow for fear you're dead? Or your father driving himself mad with worry?"

"I've neither mother nor father," Barbara said, glad to be able to tell the whole truth on this point, at least. "The relatives who brought me up did so out of charity, not fondness. Many times they've threatened to turn me loose on the world to make my own living. And this time, sir, there was just no bearing it. So I ran away. Believe me, they won't be sorry!"

"Very well. You're dressed and ready now? Then catch up with George, for he'll want you to lead his spare horse."

Without another word he turned and went, leaving Barbara to pick her way through the crowd on the beach towards Lieutenant Symonds and his two horses. She passed cake-sellers, beer-sellers, apple-sellers, and women who glanced at her incuriously, though the looks they exchanged with the older men were far from indifferent. Barbara, assessing their rouged cheeks, dyed hair and low-cut bodices, looked at them with renewed interest, for she realised she was seeing real, live loose women for the first time.

Since the closest scrutiny failed to find them alluring in any degree whatsoever, she trudged on, deciding that the world was a very different place from her imaginings, but no less fascinating for that!

"We're to make for Ghistel," Lieutenant Symonds told her as soon as they had made their way off the beach and were beginning to cross the flat, blackened sea-marshes which stretched several miles inland. "The Captain wasn't too pleased with me at first for bringing you to look after the horses. But then he saw you with Snowcloud and changed his mind. Only don't do anything to annoy him, because Dan's got a temper, which he can lose to good effect!"

"I won't," Barbara promised. "Is it far to Ghistel, sir? Will my cousin Harry be there?"

"Sure to be. And no, it isn't far; not above ten miles, I suppose. We'll be there before nightfall."

"Ten miles," Barbara said faintly. "That seems a great way to me!"

The Lieutenant laughed. "The regiment has marched thirty-seven miles in a day – when retreating, what's more, which is the worst thing out for a soldier, as I hope you may never discover. Yes, we marched over the Galician mountains in mid-winter, when the going was so hard that the men had neither shoes for their feet nor, after a while, skin on their soles. We forded rivers, slogged through snow and ice . . . Ah, but why talk of it? We're not in retreat now, nor likely to be. We're going to *win*, bantling."

"When was that retreat, sir?"

"Five or six years ago; I wasn't much older than you are. But we covered the retreat and got the army safe to Corunna, where we embarked for England and slept for the whole of the crossing. The only things awake to converse with the sailors were the bugs – and they were big enough to speak for themselves!"

"Was that when Sir John Moore was killed?" Barbara asked. "I was very young at the time, but I remember the talk."

"Aye. He *made* the rifles, Moore did. But they've

outlived him, and brought more honour to his name.
Do you like stories, Bob?"

"Oh, yes, especially true ones," Barbara said fervently. "And now I'm living in a story. Or so it seems
to me."

"You could say that," the Lieutenant mused.
"Here, how are your feet standing up to the march?"

"Very well," Barbara said truthfully, "but Celt is
fidgeting to lengthen his stride a trifle. The trouble is
I'm not very tall and I have to trot to keep up with
him if I let him walk out, as he would wish."

"Oh, you're only a featherweight; climb on to his
back and we'll both ride, and don't let me hear you
tell anyone I'm a soft touch," Lieutenant Symonds
said, then chuckled at Barbara's valiant – and fruitless – efforts to clamber up on to the big horse's back.
"What, do you need a leg-up?"

But Barbara was successful at her next attempt,
grabbing Celt by his mane and literally swarming up
his side as though climbing a wall. And then she
settled down to cover the remainder of the ten miles
in comparative comfort.

The next time Barbara saw Captain Alleyn she was
prepared for the sight, and therefore, far less nervous. They stopped at Ghistel to find three officers
there already; Captain Hugo Pryall, a dark-haired
man with a saturnine expression, Captain Bruce
French, a harsh-voiced, red-haired man with a face
so freckled that you could not put a pin between
them, and lastly Captain Alleyn, in his shirt-sleeves,
rubbing down his mare in the stable.

He glanced up as Hannibal and Celt clattered into the yard and called, "You've made it at last then, George. I suppose you were held up by that brat you brought along. Serve you right, that's all I can say!"

He seemed in a good humour, and Barbara soon found out why.

"Never seen a billet to touch it," he remarked as soon as she and Lieutenant Symonds had led the horses into their stalls. "Look at the stables, George! Thickly laid straw, as much clover as the beasts can eat, oats for the asking; and wait till you see the food at the inn! The wine's a bit thin, perhaps, but the beer is home-brewed and very good. We're all sorry we've only got one night here, and must move on tomorrow."

Captain Pryall, leaning against the stable door watching them indolently, remarked, "And fine women, too. The serving wench would just suit you, George, if we had a little more time at our disposal. Francine, she's called, and a saucy little piece if ever I saw one."

"I say, less of that," George said, casting a harassed look towards the inn. "How you can say such a thing, even in fun, I don't know! Especially you, Hugo! You were notorious for the women you kept in the Peninsula! Don't you laugh either, Dan, for I danced with the little ladybird you kept in Madrid! So don't try to make *me* out a libertine!"

"Us? Libertines? I take the greatest exception to that remark," Captain Pryall said. He strolled across the stable and began to take Celt's saddle off, then addressed Barbara as she rubbed the animal's steaming sides. "You'll see, young 'un, how the girls throw themselves at him. By breakfast tomorrow he'll have Francine eating out of his hand!"

"Well, come into the inn with us, George, and we'll acquaint you with your room and with Francine," Captain Alleyn said. "This horrid brat has been brought to look after our horses; let him do so."

"True," the red-haired Captain said. "What's your name, lad?"

"Bob, sir," Barbara said, tugging at her shako in imitation of Lew back home.

"Very well, Bob. You will sleep in the hayloft over this stable, in company with one Tobias Corklin, who is a little less green than your good self, and a good deal nastier, I daresay. However, Toby is the orphaned son of the late Sergeant Corklin; we put up with his thieving and wickedness because he has a way with horses. You'd best make friends with him — he's twelve, much your own age."

"I'm fourteen," Barbara said "I'm a bit small, but I'm fourteen."

"You are? I'd never have guessed it! Don't tell Toby, or he'll tease the hide off you. Come up to the kitchen later and you can have some supper, I daresay. If the horses have been properly groomed, that is. All of 'em!"

Barbara looked from Captain French's freckled countenance to the long line of stalls and sighed, but remembering the advice she had been given, merely said, "Yes, sir."

Captain French grinned, relenting. "Most of these nags aren't ours, so don't despair. I've done my own prads and so has Dan here. Toby saw to Hugo's before disappearing. No, you just finish Hannibal and Celt, and you can have a meal. Very likely you'll meet Toby too, if he's back from whatever devilment he's up to by then!"

The officers strolled out of the stable, leaving Barbara to the contemplation of her lot. Apart from the unknown Tobias, it did not seem too bad. The officers she had met so far – with the exception, she quickly reminded herself, of Captain Alleyn, who was a libertine and a disturber of innocent young women – seemed pleasant. She had always loved horses, and much of her youth had been spent hanging around the stables at Ulverstone Grange, helping, or hindering, the work which went on there.

She finished grooming Hannibal and stood back to admire him. Yes, the great beast looked good, despite his dip and the dusty journey. She strolled along the stalls admiring the horses, and reaching Snowcloud's gleaming hindquarters, went in and petted the mare, fondling the soft muzzle which delicately searched her pockets for titbits.

"Nothing now, my beauty, but I'll bring you back some of my supper." She investigated the ladder leading to the loft and found that Lieutenant Symonds, ever thoughtful, had put her carpet bag down at the foot of it, with her cloak folded on top.

Having finished her inspection she decided to go over to the inn and was soon comfortably installed in a corner of the dining room where the officers were eating, a plateful of stew and dumplings before her, a tall glass of ale near at hand.

Rather to her relief no one took the slightest notice of her but, quietly observant, she soon found out quite a lot about them. Bruce French was a gentle creature despite his harsh voice, and Hugo Pryall was impatient and sarcastic. Francine moved quickly round the table, understanding only one word in ten but smiling, smiling, her brown hands deft with the dishes, her eyes sliding from face to face, knowing the men admired her and enjoying their admiration.

Presently, when the table had been cleared, Daniel leaned back in his chair, took out his pipe, and said lazily, "Hugo, you've been here a while. What's new?"

"Everything," Hugo said. "What a collection will face Boney, when battle commences! Half of 'em don't know how to fire a musket or use a camp kettle!"

"What's old Nosey doing about it?" Daniel enquired. His pipe was now going to his satisfaction and he directed a long stream of smoke up at the ceiling, following it with his eyes. "Don't tell me he's leaving the decisions to his allies, for that I can't believe."

"No, the Duke's taking steps to put things right. Our army is being spread thin, like a little butter over a lot of bread, to cover every brigade of Johnny Newcomes with an experienced force. He's putting his veterans where they can do most good. He's even split *the* division, as you'll speedily find when we reach Ghent. And from there we shall move about the country a bit, to grow accustomed to one another. Manoeuvres, you know."

Daniel grinned, and blew a derisive smoke-ring at Hugo's head.

"So a mixture of raw recruits and seasoned Peninsular veterans will face Boney, eh? Well, we were all green once. I daresay we'll manage."

"Aye, for sometimes a recruit will march in where a veteran knows better than to tread," Hugo agreed. "The Duke knows what he's doing, eh, Dan?"

"None better. If anyone can knit such a force together, he can."

Quiet as a mouse in her corner, Barbara watched Captain Alleyn's lean, lively face as the talk went on. Soon, worn out by her day's adventures, she dozed, half-waking once to a shout of laughter, once to the realisation that a very improper story was being related by a deep well-remembered voice. And then George was nudging her and she was staggering, half asleep still, across the yard and into the stables, to crawl up the ladder and into a nest of sweet-smelling hay, where she fell asleep again immediately, as soundly as if she had been in her own bed at Ulverstone Grange.

CHAPTER
FOUR

BARBARA was awoken, it seemed barely ten minutes later, by a heavy weight on her chest. As she sluggishly returned to consciousness she realised that someone was shaking her, and shaking her hard, what was more.

She opened her eyes to find a face within inches of her own. A rosy-cheeked, cherubic face, framed with soft yellow hair. But at the moment the face's expression was far from cherubic, being reflective of a mixture of malice and envy.

"Lazy toad!" The words came out in a sort of growling squeak which struck Barbara, even in her uncomfortable position, as funny. "Don't you grin at me, you lazy, good-for-nothing, pot-bellied, beer-swilling, gut-rotting . . ."

"Stubble it!" Barbara said quickly, remembering her role. "Get off my chest, you nasty little boy, or I'll . . ." she hesitated, "Or I'll give you a right crack in the bread-basket."

"Little boy! That's rich, comin' from you!" Her tormentor rolled off her chest and stood over her, fists raised in a workmanlike way. "Get up, you *nasty little boy*, and I'll give you pepper!"

Barbara reflected for a moment, then struggled to

her feet. Without giving herself time to think she whirled round on Tobias – for it must be he – and knocked him flat on to the hay with flailing fists, though not without receiving a kick on the shins and a couple of frantic blows in the region of her own 'bread-basket'.

Standing triumphantly over the fallen foe, she said breathlessly, "Well?"

Tobias got to his feet, saying mildly, "Cor, what a temper! But you can't deny you tried to tek my place!"

"Of course I can deny it! And do! I'm here to help you, you chucklehead. There must be work enough for two, goodness knows."

Tobias grinned. "Aye, there is. Specially when I goes off for a bit of fun an' gig, like. You could cover for me then, if you would."

"Of course I would," Barbara said readily. "You just say the word. Though I'm the elder you were here first, after all."

"Quite a little gentry-cove, aren't you?" Tobias said cheerfully, but without malice. "You were 'ere first, after all," he mimicked. "Ne'er mind, Bob. Shall us fettle the prads before breakfast? They give us prime vittles 'ere." He sniggered. "That fat mort, the one what owns the inn, thinks I need feedin' up."

"Does she? Good!" Barbara said. She had slept in her shirt, but now pulled her jacket on and sat down in the hay to don her shoes. "Which horses shall I do, Toby? You'd best tell me, for I've no idea who owns which!"

Fortunately, Barbara's whirlwind attack seemed

to have dispersed all Tobias's grievances and the two of them worked amicably on the horses so that less than forty minutes later their job was done, and they set off for the inn kitchen in very good charity with one another.

"If we goes on workin' like this, they'll think theirselves in heaven," Tobias confided as they squared their elbows before the huge breakfast their doting hostess seemed to think necessary for growing lads. "Cor, what a feed, eh? This'll put hairs on your chest!"

He thought the remark amusing, but found Barbara's hilarity unusually prolonged for what was, after all, an old and threadbare jest. But she stopped giggling and snorting into her ale after a while and they ate steadily. And indeed, when Tobias saw her plate every bit as shinily empty as his own, his respect for his new friend grew.

"You can put back the vittles wi' the best," he admitted as they returned to the stable to saddle up. "Cor, wait till the officers sees you! They tell *me* I'll eat meself square, but you can't 'alf put it away!" He caught hold of Hannibal's saddle and staggered back to the horse's side with it. "I dunno why it is, but you look sort of frail to me. Can you manage Celt's tackle?"

Barbara could, though only by a dint of gritting her teeth and heaving did she get the saddle up on to the huge back. And as soon as they had saddled the horses, they were joined by the officers who proceeded to mount without more ado, adjuring Toby and Bob, over their shoulders, to lead the spare horses with the baggage in the saddlebags, and follow the road to Ghent.

"The regiment's at Ghent," Tobias informed his companion as they mounted the baggage ponies and took the spare horses' halters. "A good enough place, I dessay. We'll be there a while, an' you'll meet everyone."

"I've a cousin who's a subaltern with the regiment," Barbara said eagerly. "Harry Kimberley his name is. Do you know him?"

"*Course* I does! Knows the lot of 'em, don't I!" Tobias then rather spoiled this sweeping statement by adding, "Little dark chap, wiv a phizz like a bulldog? Or fat, wiv a stammer?"

"Neither. Harry's tall and fair, with curls. He's got a merry face."

"Oh, *him*. Aye, I know 'im. Johnny Newcome," Toby said laconically. "Talks of nothin' but horses, and wimmin, and hunting!"

"Oh!" Barbara blinked. "Well, he is a keen rider to hounds."

Tobias laughed. "Well, if he teks you under his wing I'll be goshswoggled! He ain't that sort, cousin or no cousin. But the Captain's worth three of the Lieutenant,.and he teks care of us."

After that, the warmth of the sun and the dust which rose chokingly from the ponies' feet discouraged further conversation. Barbara followed Tobias's lead and tied a handkerchief loosely round her nose and chin and they rode on together, through the sunny afternoon.

"Hi! Where's Toby?"

Barbara, exhaustedly grooming Hannibal, jumped and looked round. Standing in the stable doorway, peering into the gloom, was Harry. She felt her heart give a leap and knew that it was partly relief for now, at last, she would be able to share her secret with a sympathetic listener. However, she had no intention of blurting out her identity in so public a place, so she merely said, "Toby? He's gone off somewhere. He did his share first, though."

"If he did, it's unlike him," Harry grumbled. He came a little further into the stable. "Look, Captain Alleyn's found a place down by the river, where you may water the horses and let them graze. He wants Hannibal, Black Celt, Snowcloud and Santander taken down there now, and the others may go tomorrow." He looked at her uncertainly in the dimness. "Can you manage all four?"

"No, of course I can't," Barbara said. "If you bring Snowcloud and Santander, though, I can manage the other two."

"Hey, I've got better things to do than . . ."

"Then find Toby, or tell Captain Alleyn to water his own horses," Barbara said equably.

Harry, after a moment's indecision, turned into Snowcloud's stall, a scowl marring his smooth brow, and presently, as she led George's two horses across the yard, she heard the clop of hooves behind her and knew that Harry was following suit.

Once by the river, she let Hannibal and Celt walk into the water up to their knees and stand there, muzzles just touching the surface, eagerly drinking the cool amber liquid. Only then did she turn and confront Harry, who had already released Snowcloud and Santander and was standing on the bank waiting for her and obviously itching to give her a piece of his mind.

· "Now look here, you young looby, I don't intend to take my orders from *you*, so you'd best see that in future it's the other way round. I put up with enough sauce from young Toby, so I won't take . . . take . . . ."

Barbara had moved towards him as his tirade continued, until there was scarcely a foot between them. His voice trailed away and he gazed at her, open-mouthed. "Hello, Harry," she murmured. "Are you glad to see me?"

He turned sickly pale; passing a hand across his brow. "Babs? *Can* it be you? Dear God, what are you doing here? And in lad's rig!"

"Who else? Oh Harry, it's a long story! Have I time to tell you now? Is there any fear of our being interrupted?"

Harry, recovering his complexion a little, turned and led her into the shade of some big willow trees which grew close to the bank. "The officers have all gone into Ghent," he said. "I was to have gone, but you . . . he . . . you saddled me with the horses." There was enough resentment in his voice to cause Barbara a moment's dismay; did he not want her, now that she had come so far?

Once in the shelter of the trees, however, curiosity got the better of whatever annoyance he was still harbouring over forgoing his trip to Ghent. "Well?" he demanded.

"Well, an old gentleman, a friend of my father's, made me an offer of marriage, which my uncle Landrake said I must accept. So I ran away, of course. I went to Harwich and searched for you, and then George Symonds found me and told me you were in Belgium. What could I *do*, Harry? I had to find you, didn't I, for I could not marry an old man when I am promised to you! But anyway, Lieutenant Symonds took care of me and now we're together. Everything will be all right, won't it? You do want to marry me, don't you?"

"I can't possibly marry you just like that, particularly in Belgium," Harry said, a hunted expression crossing his face. "This is a Catholic country, full of priests. And what about . . . well, this Bob Garland? You're a boy as far as the company is concerned."

"Bob would just have to disappear," Barbara said, not without regret. "Other people have wives, Harry. Lots and lots of wives are here with their husbands. I was surprised, I must say. Oh, I knew there would be camp-followers because you told me, but I didn't know that Colonels and Majors and so on would bring their wives and sometimes their babies, out here with them. I assure you it is so!"

"But not subalterns," Harry said, a note of distaste creeping into his voice. "Definitely not subalterns. Good God, Babs, I'm only learning my trade as yet, I can't take on a wife, and brats too, like as not, in a year or so! It would be different if we were at home, of course, but . . ."

"You did say we'd marry when you were twenty-one," Barbara pointed out patiently. "But if you don't want to marry me, I still had no choice but to run away. I shall just have to remain Bob Garland until this big battle which everyone says will come is over. I'm making myself very useful, Harry. You'll just have to forget I was ever Babs and treat me as Bob, as the others do."

"It isn't . . . I didn't mean I didn't want to marry you," stammered the hapless Harry. "For I do! But in peacetime, Babs, and in England. What's more, if my parents ever got wind of this latest prank they'd never consent to our marriage, never. Imagine Mamma's face, seeing you in breeches and a shako!" His fair brows came together. "Honestly, Babs, this time you've gone too far! Your reputation would be ruined if it came out, for you must have been sleeping with the rest of the servants and grooms, I suppose?"

There was enough prurient curiosity in his voice to set Barbara's hackles up, but she said offhandedly, "I've been billeted with Toby, of course. We sleep in the haylofts, so I just roll myself in my blanket. I see no harm in that."

Harry had the grace to look a little ashamed of himself. "That's all right, I suppose. But what story shall you tell in England? They're bound to ask, even if you go back within the next two or three days."

"I'm not going back," Barbara said. "I told you, Harry, that if I went back to Uncle Landrake he'd insist on my marrying the old man. If you won't marry me, then I'll stay here until I find myself some respectable occupation." She sighed, realising as never before the difficulty of her position. "It has all turned out quite differently from how I planned it," she finished forlornly.

"Well, it isn't my fault," Harry said defensively. "When I left you'd not a care in the world! If you ask me, Babs, you'd have done better to accept the old fellow. After all, he wouldn't have married you out of hand, you could have played for time! And even when I'm of age, there's no saying my father would support me and my wife. And we could scarcely live on a subaltern's pay!"

"I wish you'd never talked of marriage if you didn't mean it," Barbara said, her face hot with humiliation. "I was a fool, just like Elmira said. She told me you were only flirting, and had no intention of marrying me."

"Well, I did mean it," Harry said, his colour as high as her own. "Only . . . only not so *soon*, Babs! And not like this, in a hole-and-corner way. I meant to court you in style when I came home, with Lord Landrake's consent. We could have been betrothed for a while – that sort of thing. As it is, I don't know what to do for the best. You ought to go home, of course, but I suppose you wouldn't go back to Ulverstone Grange now, and what to do with you other than that fairly perplexes me!"

"Just leave me alone," Barbara said. "I've been a stupid chit, and I'm sorry I've embarrassed you. Just leave me alone, Harry."

Harry caught her hand. "I'll tell you what! You get yourself some quiet, genteel sort of employment and we'll brush round it, I promise you that. How about your going as nursemaid to Lady Hollins? I'm sure she's advertised enough times, for her girls are always leaving her. Her children are so abominably spoilt, you see."

"Who would have me as a nursemaid with my hair cut short, and when I can give them no good reason for my being in Belgium and dare not admit I'm related to Lord Landrake? It's no use, Harry, I shall have to remain a boy until I return to England."

Harry looked sulky. "Then you must move from my regiment. How can I treat you like a stableboy when I know you're really Barbara Campion? It won't work you know, Babs. I'd not feel easy."

Barbara stared into Harry's stormy blue eyes. For the first time, she realised just how thoroughly spoilt and selfish her old friend was. He thought nothing of her feelings; of her, a girl, having to face the difficulties and indeed dangers of joining another regiment, making new friends, perhaps being at the mercy of a lieutenant who disliked her or, worse, guessed her secret.

For a moment he met her gaze, then his eyes dropped. He said sulkily, "I can't force you to change your regiment, but you might think of *me* for once. Suppose Dan or Hugo or one of the others found out you're a girl? Do you think they'd imagine for one moment that I was innocent? They'd think . . . I can't bring myself to consider it."

He turned all his charm on her suddenly, smiling winningly at her. "Come on, Babs, be a sport! I'll find you a good place in another regiment, I swear I will!"

Barbara eyed him steadily. "No, Harry. I won't

join another regiment, but I won't embarrass you by watching your amours, if that's what you fear! And I won't mention marriage again, I can promise you that! I'm going to take Hannibal and Celt back to their stable now."

She turned her back on him and caught Hannibal's headstall. The big horse was reluctant to leave the sweet grass, but he had been well trained and Celt, drowsing in the shallows, joined his stable companion without demur.

Behind her, Barbara heard without sympathy Harry's cries as he tried to persuade Snowcloud and Santander to let him catch them. Serve him right, she thought vindictively. But before she had reached the stables, her plight had brought tears to her eyes and when Harry eventually caught her up, in the stables, drying down Celt's gleaming flanks, one glance at her face was enough to bring him to her side.

He put his arms round her shoulders and gave her a squeeze. "Silly chicken," he said remorsefully. "I've behaved like a selfish brute, because I've been spoiled to death at home and told I'm always right, and must always have my own way! But I'm learning differently here, I promise you. I'm sorry, Babs, and ashamed. There! It will work out, you see. And I won't *let* you join another company, not if you was to beg me!"

Barbara gave a gargantuan sniff and a watery giggle. "I knew I couldn't be so mistaken in you," she said shyly. "And I won't embarrass you; here's my hand on it."

Solemnly they shook hands, and Harry said, "You make a most convincing boy, Babs! Strange, because you're the prettiest chit in your petticoats! Now I'd best be off, or there will be stories about my hanging round the stables." He walked towards the doorway, then turned. "I say, you don't know which is my prad, do you? He's a stallion, so watch yourself near his hindquarters for he can lash out, I tell you. His name's Taffy, and he's a chestnut. Mind you take good care of him!"

Laughing, he made his way out into the sunshine of the yard. Barbara watched as the tall, gold-topped figure in the well-cut green uniform was swallowed up by the farmhouse, and then she turned back to the stable. There was feed to fetch, and when the officers got back from Ghent there would be more horses to water. She really ought to find out what Tobias was up to, and she must dry the horses' legs and brush off the mud.

There was no doubt about it, even without the complication of Harry's being unable to marry her quite yet, life was full. She made for the ladder leading into the loft. She might as well sleep for an hour or so, until it was time for the evening meal and settling the horses down for the night. They would be on the road early tomorrow, Captain Alleyn had said.

"We're making our way towards Brussels," Harry had told Barbara in a quiet aside the previous evening. "They have had a grand time in Brussels, I've heard. Balls every night, and the prettiest women to dance with! But we've missed most of that, for the Duke is getting restive. Mark my words, we shall settle down into our quarters and no sooner have we done so than we'll be sent out scouting for the French, noting villages and rivers, taking the lie of the land, measuring the depth of every blessed duckpond so that when Nosey stands, he stands at the sort of position he enjoys for a battle."

Now, marching along the road with the troops in front kicking up a terrible dust, Barbara was glad that at least she knew where she was going, and to what sort of situation. She had watched Harry go off, riding beside the company with as much panache as though he were already the captain he longed to be. He looked so magnificent that she could scarcely forbear to cheer, and thought him quite the handsomest of men.

How was it, therefore, she asked herself as she and Toby rode in the rear of the column, that when Captain Alleyn rode up on Snowcloud in his old, stained uniform, with his eyes narrowed against the glare and his face grim, the men cheered him? She supposed vaguely that they had known him longer. She sternly repressed her own brief flicker of feeling that here was the better man. After all, she knew that however good a soldier Alleyn might be, he was a libertine who took advantage of poverty-stricken little girls!

The day's march was a long one, but when it ended, in a little village square, she was pleased to find herself as fresh as Tobias, though that was not saying much!

"We'll feed an' water the prads before we gets us any prog," groaned Toby, gazing hopefully up at Captain Alleyn. "That is, unless you says otherwise!"

The Captain laughed, but did not relent. "Look to the horses, and then you may stuff yourselves with good things, if there are good things available. But billets are going to be rare once we're forming battle fronts. Can either of you cook?"

"I can," Barbara said, "simple stuff."

"Good. I'll remind you of that when we're billeted in some miserable hovel, with only our rations to make us a meal." He grinned down at her, slapping her shoulder so hard that she winced. "Only bamming you! There will be none of that here, for the country is rich and the peasants only too willing to have us billeted upon them. We pay, unlike the French! We're in another farmhouse tonight; the food's always good in farmhouses, and the stable loft cosy."

Only one occurrence that day was regrettable and that was when, dusty and tired from their journey and from working on the horses, she and Toby went into the kitchen for their meal. Captain Alleyn was there, with Harry and George.

"What a pair of horrid brats," Captain Alleyn remarked. "Toby, when did you last wash? And you, Bob?"

Barbara felt her face crimsoning.

"Yesterday? I don't believe a word of it," Captain Alleyn said. "You're black, the pair of you. Wash, or there'll be no supper."

"Right you are, sir," Toby said with deceptive readiness. "I'll pump for you, Bob, and then you can pump for me."

"No need," Captain Alleyn said. "I'll pump for you both. Out with you Toby, and strip off that shirt. And you, Bob!"

Barbara sensed Harry's sudden stillness before he said calmly, "Pair of sweeps in truth, aren't they, Dan? But don't bother yourself; I'll pump for 'em, and make sure they're clean before they eat."

Time stood still for Barbara while Captain Alleyn, brows raised, stared at Harry, then said, "Good of you. Very well, pump away."

The three of them went out into the yard. Harry said, beneath his breath, "What'll you do, Babs? He'll be watching. If you don't take your shirt off, he'll either come out here and take it off for you, or start to suspect."

"Make Toby wash first," Barbara hissed. "Oh God, these light evenings! If only it were dark!"

But Tobias, happily, created a diversion, for no sooner was his shirt off than he leaped for the safety of the stable. Barbara, acting with what she devoutly hoped would merely be taken for promptness, ran straight under the water fully dressed, then struggled out of her wet shirt and, keeping her back to the farmhouse, clutched the wet shirt to her, letting the cold water swish and patter on to her hunched shoulders and back for a moment. Then, still with the shirt strategically held, she bounded, shivering, into the stables.

"Toby!" she called up the ladder. "You'd best get

into the yard. The Captain won't be pleased." There was no reply. Speaking in her most persuasive tones, Barbara called, "Toby! Don't you want your supper? I'm starving!"

There was a rustling, then a round-eyed face with a halo of yellow hair peered down at her. "I'm 'ollow as a drum," Toby said pathetically. "But I 'ates being pumped! Don't you?"

Barbara giggled at his choice of phrase but agreed fervently that, in future, she would make sure she was clean before the Captain spotted her.

"Don't you fink the Captain'll get tired of waiting?" Toby said hopefully.

Barbara sighed. She could not very well climb up into the loft in her half-naked state and put on a clean shirt whilst Toby remained up there! "No, I'm sure he won't. On the other hand, the farmer's wife may very well give our supper to someone else."

There was a silence whilst Toby digested this, and then a voice calling his name from the yard decided him. Giving a deep sigh, he climbed slowly down the ladder. Barbara, her arms round her damp shirt, saw him leave the stable with lagging steps and then charged up the ladder, and within a very short time was back in the kitchen once more, her wet hair neatly combed, her clean shirt sparkling at her throat, her uniform jacket firmly fastened.

Captain Alleyn smiled at her, then glanced towards the stable yard, one eyebrow raised interrogatively.

"He's under the pump now," Barbara said, taking her place at the table. "Can't you *hear* him?"

Captain Alleyn cocked his head, then winced as a gurgling shriek rent the air. "He can't swim as well as you," he said mildly, as Barbara grinned. "Nor, I imagine, has he had your education."

"I don't see that being educated makes washing under a pump any pleasanter," Barbara objected, as the farmer's wife ladled thick pea soup into her dish.

"Don't you? Well, I assure you it does! Toby sees no good in cleanliness, whereas you, well-educated young fellow that you are, know that it is healthier, for one thing, to be clean. Though why you should choose to have your wash with your shirt also under the jet, I can't imagine."

Barbara disguised a slight jump at this unexpected attack by coughing, hand to mouth. "I . . . I . . ." she began, then pulled herself together. Raising limpid eyes to his quizzical face, "It needed washing, sir."

"To be sure," he nodded. "Just as it did in the sea, at Ostend."

Barbara could feel the colour flooding her face, but she continued to meet his eyes. "That was an accident," she said. "But I admit, sir, that I've led a . . . a sheltered life. That's to say, I never went away to school, nor did I mix with other . . . other boys of my age. Perhaps I'm too self-conscious to relish stripping. I – I'm very *thin*, and . . ."

But he was turning away. "You'll grow less self-conscious," he threw over his shoulder as he quitted the room. "Especially when we bathe in the river, as we shall if this fine weather continues. You swim well, perhaps your love of the sport will overcome a natural shyness."

Barbara bent her burning face over her soup, spooning it into her mouth and trying to think of a good excuse for not bathing in the river. Should she strain her back? Break a leg? Commit suicide, perhaps? She had to laugh at her own frantic thoughts. There was no point in worrying; after all, no one could make her join the officers in the river, and she was very sure that Toby would do no such thing. Probably Captain Alleyn was only teasing, after all!

CHAPTER
FIVE

"WE'VE done well here, Bob, and tomorrow we move on. I shall be sorry to leave this place, but we'll be quartered just outside Brussels, so we shall see something of the city, and you may see the Duke of Wellington at last. You'll like that, for it is annoying to hear so much about the great man when you've never set eyes on him."

Daniel Alleyn stood, absently patting Snow-cloud's gleaming neck, whilst Barbara poured bran mash into the manger.

"Yes, I want to see the Duke, and Brussels," she said now. "Does that mean that the battle is imminent, do you think?"

The Captain shrugged. "Who can tell? But I think the Duke intends to stand between Brussels and the French. Our spies have been bringing in news of Napoleon's army, but I'm sure the French have better informants than we. When news from France dries up, then there will be action, and I think that'll happen within the next couple of weeks. Why, are you worried? You will be with the spare horses and all the baggage you know, to the rear and out of the fighting."

Barbara set the empty bucket down and raised her

hand to smooth Snowcloud's rippling mane. "I'm not worried . . ." she began.

Then it happened.

From the dim rafters overhead a huge spider suddenly descended, landing with scrabbling legs on Barbara's bare arm. Ever since she could remember, Barbara had been terrified of spiders, the very sight of them bringing blind, atavistic fear so strong that she lost all control of her actions.

Now her shriek and upflung arm made Snowcloud plunge and rear, and Barbara, stumbling blindly away, put her foot in the feed bucket, and crashed almost under the restless hooves. Captain Alleyn shouted and the spider, suddenly finding itself hurtling through the air, landed and proceeded to run with horrid agility over the straw, straight towards Barbara's terrified face.

She had a muddled picture of the spider, looking the size of a crab, making at her, all mixed up with Captain Alleyn vaulting over Snowcloud's back, and the mare's hooves, which had been dancing within inches of her face, suddenly moving away as the Captain pushed against her.

But the spider was still advancing and Barbara's ear-splitting scream made Snowcloud sidle and dance, and even as her hooves came within inches of Barbara's head hard hands seized her and pulled her to safety.

Safety from death beneath Snowcloud's nervous hooves, that is; the spider was still heading in her direction. "Kill it, kill it!" Barbara implored, clutching the Captain's arms. She shuddered, pressing herself back against his chest, forgetting everything except that the enemy was almost upon her.

"What? What?" Daniel demanded, thoroughly bewildered. "Pull yourself together, Bob! What happened? Did Snowcloud bite you?" He became aware of her shudders and patted her soothingly as one might a nervous horse. "Gently, lad, gently. You're quite safe!"

The spider, confused by the noise and the restless hooves, had frozen into a beady stillness. Barbara, made reckless by fear, squeaked, "Oh, sir! It's there, look! Take it away, do! I . . . I . . ."

Captain Alleyn, his arm still round her shoulders, followed her pointing finger. "A *spider*? All that noise and fuss over a spider?" Nevertheless he stepped forward and trod heavily on the offending creature. "Confound it, Bob, what sort of a man will you make if a spider causes you to throw the stables into confusion? Do you know you were almost killed just now?" His annoyance was growing as he realised the harm such irrational behaviour might have caused. "Bob, have you *no* sense? Suppose you'd been in ambush and a spider had appeared? Would you have shrieked out like that, letting every Frenchman for miles know your whereabouts? You could cause the death of your companions as well as yourself by such foolishness."

He was working himself up into a rage, for when he had seen Snowcloud's hooves so close to the soft dark curls a most unpleasant sensation of helplessness had gripped him, and even now reaction was making his hands tremble.

"Indeed, I can't help it, sir," Barbara said plaintively. "It was *on* me, on my skin," she added, as though the explanation made everything quite clear.

"I don't care if it was doing the waltz up and down your legs, you've got to cure yourself of making such a fuss," the Captain said harshly. He drew back from her, eyeing her measuringly. "I've a good mind to take a whip to you, you young ninny! You're no better than a girl, though, so I'll content myself with this."

He swung her round by one shoulder and before she could protest or escape she was bent across his knee, and his hand was descending with relentless regularity on the seat of her breeches.

It hurt, but Barbara knew better than to shout or wriggle, and after a dozen hard, stinging blows he stood her upright.

"I hope that will make you think twice before you fuss over trifles again," he said breathlessly. "Next time, if there is a next time, I'll take a riding whip to you."

"I'm sorry," Barbara mumbled, her face red from being upside down, her eyes watering from the forceful spanking she had received. "I won't shout again."

"I should hope not. If you shriek over a spider, you'd shriek twice as loud over a whipping. Get on with your work."

Barbara, her hands straying to her tingling rear, bent obediently and picked up the bucket, but could not resist saying, as Daniel made for the stable door,

72

"But you must admit, Captain Alleyn, that I didn't so much as yelp over the beating, so very likely it's only spiders which make me shriek."

He turned, one eyebrow raised. "Perhaps I didn't beat you hard enough," he said grimly. "Don't answer me back, boy!"

Barbara, obediently mixing bran mash and carrying it to each horse in turn, thought that if anything could cure her of screaming at spiders, it was the threat of being whipped. But that did not make her regard Captain Alleyn with any more fondness!

"Well, we're off to Brussels at last," Harry said. He spoke ostensibly to Hugo Pryall, but Barbara knew the words were directed at herself. "We shall see some fun there, I don't doubt."

Toby, standing in the stableyard holding the baggage ponies, whilst all around them the officers were preparing to leave, said *sotto voce* to Barbara, "*They may see some fun, but we shan't.*"

Barbara smiled sympathetically at him. Toby was in trouble, not for the first time it transpired, with Captain Alleyn.

"Says I prigged the pearl beads off that fat old mort," Toby had said contemptuously. "What a fing to say! An' I give 'em back, din't I, soon as he said I must?"

"He shouldn't have beaten you," Barbara said now. "But I daresay he thinks if we're harshly treated we shall behave better." She had confided in Toby that she had been beaten, but had been vague as to the cause since she foresaw endless spider attacks if the urchin ever discovered her fear.

Toby, however, took offence at her remark. "Harsh? Cor, you don't know the 'alf! My Pa would 'ave took the skin off me back, not just dusted me jacket for me!"

"Oh! But you said the Captain had marked you," Barbara said, slightly taken aback by this sudden change of attitude.

The horses were moving now, and Toby nudged the baggage pony into motion with his heels. "Marked me? Course I said 'e marked me! I like 'im to fink I'm easily hurt, see. You should always jump an' holler when you're hit! Then they fink they're 'alf killin' you, see? Didn't you shout when he beat you?"

"Well, no," Barbara said, admiring Toby's display of low cunning. She added hastily, foreseeing a lecture, "But I will, now that you've explained."

"Good," Toby said. " 'Cos if you act like the iron man they'll 'it you as if you was. See?"

Barbara admitted that she saw, and they rode some way in silence. Ahead of them, the column marched steadily on, the officers riding their horses up and down beside the men, chatting first to one and then another.

The hours passed. The countryside was beautiful, with pretty little villages set, gem-like, amidst the woods and gently rolling hills.

Presently Harry, coming back along the column, slowed beside them. "Nearly there," he said cheerfully. "From up ahead I can see Brussels."

"Oh, good," Barbara said thankfully. "Where are we to be billeted, Lieutenant?"

"A small village, not far off. The officers will be at a farm and you two lads will be above the stables. The men will scatter amongst the cottages. And tonight, the captain says, we may go into the city. There's plenty going on there, from all accounts."

"Can *we* go in?" Barbara said eagerly. "Me and Toby, I mean?"

Harry shrugged, wheeling his horse around again. "I don't know about that. Wait and see."

Toby stared after him, his expression baleful. "When 'e talks to you, 'e sounds quite human," he observed. "But 'e doesn't like me, doesn't 'is lordship!"

"Well, he's my cousin," Barbara said defensively. "Why do you say he doesn't like you?"

"He picks on me," Toby stated. "When 'e first joined, it was ' 'On took me silver backed 'airbrushes? 'Oo took me best linen shirt? 'Oo took me 'namelled snuff box?' But since you've got 'ere, he's been better."

"Well, that's not picking on you," Barbara observed. "Because the chances are you did take them!"

"Oh, I din't say nuffing about not taking 'em," Toby admitted. "Blimey, I got 'alf a thick 'un for the 'airbrushes! I just said 'e picked on me."

Barbara, deciding that Toby's logic was beyond her, merely grunted, and presently they found themselves in the stableyard of a sizeable farmhouse, with men all round them, and Captain Alleyn shouting at them to "Get the horses cleaned down and fed and be quick about it, for we want to ride into Brussels after we've dined."

The two youngsters made their way into the stables, and were immediately impressed by the size and cleanliness of the place, and by the enormous horses already in residence.

"That's a Percheron," Barbara said, pointing to a heavy draught horse with a silky grey coat and a pair of mildly enquiring brown eyes. "And that one, in the next stall, is a Brabançon; isn't he *vast*, Toby? They're specially bred for the claggy, heavy soil round these parts, I believe. And the red roan further along is a Boulonnais, I think; they're useful carriage horses I believe, because although they're big they've got a certain elegance." She moved into the stall, and patted the gleaming russet neck. "Grand fellow, aren't you?"

"Why've they got so many breeds, and 'ow come you know 'em?" Toby asked curiously as they walked further down the stalls. "To me, a prad is a prad!"

"My uncle breeds draught horses, and I've always been interested," Barbara said. "I imagine this farmer must breed too, since he has so many." She paused by another stall. "This plain-looking bay is an Ardennes; ugly fellow, isn't he, with his cropped mane, and short legs supporting that heavy body? But there's nothing like 'em for stamina. They went to Russia with Napoleon, you know, and that's made them well known, for they withstood that terrible weather, the hardships, everything. But there, I mustn't forget *you're* the expert on horses."

"Not like that, though," Toby said, looking at Barbara with awe. "I say, Bob, would you teach us, eh? All them names an' that. What each prad does, 'ow to tell 'em apart, and so on?"

"Yes, of course I will," Barbara said readily. "But we'd best get our own prads, as you call them, cleaned up, or we won't get any supper. And after, Toby, let *us* go into Brussels!"

Usually, Toby was apt to slope off on business of his own the moment they arrived at a new billet, but perhaps the beating he had received from the Captain had made him chary of 'slumming the ken', which Barbara gathered meant seeing what he could steal. Anyway, when they'd finished with the horses and seen the officers go riding merrily down the road they got themselves a good supper, and then stole out to the stable, put bridles on the baggage ponies, and set off down the road into Brussels.

"Phew!" Barbara remarked, as they slid off the ponies and tethered them to a post in a quiet side street. "Don't your legs get tired, though, riding bareback?"

"A bit," acknowledged Toby. "Come on, where'll we go?"

"Well, away from here," Barbara said, wrinkling her nose. "What an awful smell! I suppose it comes from that fish market but I must say it puts me off fish. And the town looked so beautiful as we approached, but these horrible black stone cottages aren't as I'd imagined it to be at all."

"We'll go into the centre," Toby said. "The officers went to some place where there's dancing. Look, I'll ask."

With the sublime confidence of one who had managed to make himself understood across half Europe, Toby banged on the nearest door. Nor was his confidence misplaced, for he came hurrying back presently, saying, "Follow me! There's a big party for the nobs and that feller told me where to go. Shift yourself."

Barbara obediently fell into step beside him and presently they found themselves in a wide, tree-lined square where a number of dark green uniforms could be seen, mingling with the scarlets and blues of other regiments, and with the pale-shaded gowns of a number of ladies who looked to be both beautiful and high-born.

"Shall us watch for a bit?" Toby said glumly. "No use trying for any sport whilst they're all out 'ere."

"Yes, let's," Barbara said. She sat herself down on a low wall and stared around her, her shako tipped over her nose to avoid recognition should any of their officers happen to glance her way. She was particularly fascinated to observe that many of the young and comely women wore mantillas and black dresses, giving an exotic Spanish touch to the proceedings.

She pointed this out to Toby, who informed her at once that not only in their dress did the Bruxellaises resemble the Andalusians.

"I suppose it's because Spain colonised the Low Countries a couple of hundred years ago," Barbara concluded. "Certainly the Flemish peasants are quite different from these slender, dark-eyed beauties."

Toby sniffed. "I'm off," he said briefly. "Shan't be long."

Barbara, left alone, watched somewhat apprehensively as Toby made his way across the square. She noticed that the boy was making towards the cake and lemonade vendor whose booth made a patch of colour on the *trottoir*, and realising Toby had no money, half rose to her feet, afraid that he might intend to augment his income by picking a pocket or some other devilry. But almost at once she sank down on to the wall again for within a few feet of her, two familiar figures in rifle green were strolling. Harry and Captain Alleyn. And both — *both* had a fair partner on his arm!

Captain Alleyn was with a plump, pretty blonde with soft pink cheeks and a gurgling laugh. Barbara heard the laugh quite distinctly when the Captain put his arm around his partner's waist. And Harry, she saw with sorrow, had found himself one of the lovely Spanish-looking girls, with gentle, doe-like black eyes, smooth, dark hair, and an exquisite figure clad in a simple white muslin gown which clung provocatively to every curve.

For a moment Barbara considered returning to the farm alone. Then she took a deep breath and scolded herself. Had she not promised Harry that she would not object to his amours? And where, for goodness' sake, was the harm? He could scarcely dance with her! So why should he not dance with another? As for Captain Alleyn, he was welcome to dance with whom he pleased. The fact that he chose a fat, painted harlot with dyed hair and a transparent gown was no concern of hers. Why, she knew him already for a libertine – and a bully, who beat little boys just because they were afraid of spiders!

With these thoughts in mind, she walked discreetly behind the officers and presently saw them vanish into a tall house to one side of the square. Her impulse to continue to spy on them was strong enough to send her straight round the back. Yes, a garden, with long windows overlooking a terrace.

Without a second thought she hoisted herself up on to the high garden wall and dropped lightly into a border which, to the detriment of her breeches, seemed to consist largely of rose-bushes. However, she freed herself from the thorns and stole over to the window.

She must have taken longer than she had thought, for the couples were whirling in the dance already. There went Harry, the little beauty in his arms smiling seductively up at him. But where was Captain Alleyn? Then she saw him, on the opposite side of the room. He was not dancing but seemed to be abstractedly watching as the lively performers whirled past. Indeed, for a moment it seemed as though his eyes looked straight into hers. She drew back, startled, then realised that he could scarcely have seen her hovering in the dark, when he was in the brilliantly illuminated ballroom.

Next moment, she saw him talking earnestly to a heavily-built civilian whose nose shone unbecomingly purple in the candlelight.

She watched for a while longer, enchanted by the colour and the air of gaiety; wishing, in an obscure way, that this was the terrace of Ulverstone Grange and that presently she would be asked to waltz by some . . . some . . .

A hand, seeming to come from nowhere, caught her by the arm.

"So I *was* right! Bob, how came you . . ."

Barbara turned, her eyes widening with fright, and met Captain Alleyn's accusing gaze. And she saw, helplessly, the dawn of a double recognition glimmer in his dark eyes.

"Good God! Surely it's. . . . Come over here, child."

He pulled her away from the terrace and down into the garden. There, in a bright patch of white moonlight, he scrutinised her closely while she closed her eyes and prayed he would not challenge her.

"You're not Bob Garland. You're Cinderella," he said at last, quietly. She opened her eyes and he was standing close, looking down into her face. He shook his head in wonder at his own stupidity. "Why I didn't realise it before I can't imagine, except that I never dreamed . . ." He put his hand out and tilted her chin up, smiling quizzically into her eyes. "Why on earth did you act out such a charade?" His glance suddenly sharpened, a look of blazing eagerness lighting up his eyes. "Did you come to seek me?"

Dumbly, not understanding, she shook her head. "Then why . . ."

"I sought Harry Kimberley," she muttered. "We were . . . fond of one another. And then, my uncle talked of . . . of an arranged marriage. With someone older, you understand. So I ran away, thinking to find Harry at Harwich. But . . . but he'd sailed for Ostend. So I came too."

He said grimly, "Was the marriage so distasteful to you, then?"

"Yes, of course! How could I want to marry a man I'd never met? But Harry can't marry me; not here, not yet. And he didn't know what to do! He wanted to send me home, back to England, but I swore I wouldn't return to my uncle's house. How can I, when he would . . ."

"Force you into marriage," he concluded for her. "But back to England you must go, my little one! And back to your uncle, too! Oh, don't worry about the marriage! Now that you've made your feelings so obvious, I've no doubt your suitor will withdraw his offer. As for Harry, I take it there is no reason why he *should* marry you at once?"

Fortunately, perhaps, Barbara did not take his meaning, but said, "No, sir. He swears he wants to wed, though, when we return to England. But . . . but he thinks I've ruined my reputation and says that unless we can invent a convincing story to account for my absence, his parents will never consent to the match."

"Consent? Does he need their consent, then? He must be almost of age."

"Yes, he is, but he says we shall need his parents' help for he cannot afford to support a wife."

"Hmm. It looks as if you're in a pretty mess, Miss Campion! But I've friends in Brussels; shall I throw myself upon their charity and beg a place for you?"

"If you do, they're bound to think the worst," Barbara said frankly. She had been standing looking up into his face but now her hands went out to him appealingly. "Oh please, sir, forget you know the truth! No one has offered me the least harm and I'm doing a good job with the horses. Let me stay!"

Until he had spoken of a real possibility of turning her into a lass again and finding her a place, Barbara had not realised how she relished her new freedom. Nor how she enjoyed the company of Harry and the other officers. But now, with England a possibility, and a place, perhaps as nursemaid or governess, a reality which she might grasp, she knew she would fight with everything at her command to remain Bob Garland.

He was watching her closely, his own face unreadable in the tricky moonlight.

"But now that I know you for what you are, Cinders, won't you be sorely embarrassed in my company? For I can treat you no differently, you know, despite my knowledge. And if you allow me to speak to my friends, you may be sure of respectability, and Harry! If you want to stay with the regiment, I must warn you that tomorrow I had planned to take yourself and some officers into France, to see if we can meet up with the French army. If you came with us, you would just be Bob Garland again, sharing whatever privations and risks the rest of us endured. Now, you must make a sensible choice. Would it not be better if you remained in Brussels with some good-natured woman who sympathised with your plight? Lady Birkenshaw, the lady who walked with me in the square earlier this evening, would help, for she's got a kind heart."

I dare say she's generous to a fault, the yellow-haired jade, Barbara thought unkindly, but she had the sense not to say the words out. Aloud, she said primly, "I'll remain with the regiment, if you please. I shall be happy to go with you into France, and I shan't think about Miss Campion, so you won't embarrass me." She grinned up at him suddenly, her eyes sparkling. "Only don't, I beg you, order me under the pump!"

He grinned back, eyebrows flying up in amused recollection. "Dear God, and even then it never occurred to me." He began to chuckle softly. "And the spider! Of *course*! Why, it should have . . ."

She knew why he had broken off; he had remembered the beating. To ease the situation, she said, "Well, sir, I'm Bob again now! And I'd best return to the square and find Toby, or we shall both be discovered, and that would never do."

She turned to go but he detained her, a hand on her arm. "How did you get into the city? Not, I trust, on my spare horse?"

Barbara smiled up at him, her glance impish. "No, sir, we rode the baggage ponies. But suppose I had ridden Santander? What would you do? Beat me?"

Without waiting for a reply she slipped out of the shelter of the trees and ran lightly towards the garden wall. She heard his chuckle, then he said appreciatively. "Minx! But remember, you're Bob Garland again now – I might beat you, at that!" He walked in long strides after her, reaching the wall nearly as soon as she did. "Let me give you a leg-up."

"What, help Bob climb a wall? You underestimate me, sir. Just watch!"

She took a few steps back, measured the height with her eye, then leapt, catching at the top of the wall and bringing her wiry young muscles into play to pull herself up to the summit. She paused for a moment, her triumphant smile lingering.

"Goodnight, goodnight, parting is such sweet sorrow," she quoted, looking down on him as he stood below her, *"That I shall say goodnight till it be morrow."*

He was close under the wall. Now, with his face tilted up to hers, and his hands creeping up the bricks, he murmured, *"Sleep dwell upon thine eyes, peace in thy breast! Would I were sleep and peace, so sweet to rest."*

Barbara paused, looking down at him uncertainly. Her own words had been light and mocking, but his answer? It had been spoken in a hushed half-whisper, but she knew, suddenly, that he was quite serious. The expression on his face, lifted to hers in the moonlight, brought a sudden giddiness upon her, so that for a moment she longed to slide down the wall and into his arms.

Then she shook herself. Fool that she was, to be

taken in by the practised wooing of a man like Daniel Alleyn! No doubt as soon as she was gone he would return to the house – and whisper Shakespearian quotations into her ear of the blonde and cuddly Lady Birkenshaw!

Briskly, without allowing herself any more time to think, she dropped down into the side street, glanced round her cautiously, then made for the square. Once there, she should be able to join Toby and then they could find their way back to the ponies. But still she hesitated. Should she go back with Toby, or try to get in touch with Harry to tell him about this latest turn of events? Then, shrugging, she sauntered into the square again, hands in pockets. She would say nothing, but would wait on events. She had no desire to have Harry ring a peal over her head because she had refused Daniel's offer of a respectable position!

As she reached the square she saw Toby, leaning against a tree. She waved, and he beckoned her to join him.

"Strawberries!" he said, as soon as she was within earshot. "They was 'aving strawberries at the 'ouse the Captain went in, an' I prigged a few." He held out a generous handful. "See? Saved some for you!"

And Barbara, gobbling strawberries, found her worries receding. For she was only Bob Garland, after all. She had only to take orders, and do her best!

CHAPTER
SIX

"THE Captain *knows*? And you're still coming with us into France? Babs, does he know you followed me? He must think me the veriest rascal . . ."

Barbara and Harry were in the stable, ostensibly saddling up Harry's tall chestnut stallion whilst Barbara, in a half-whisper, confided the happenings of the previous evening. She had decided, upon reflection, that to tell Harry was her duty. Now she said, "He knows that I fled from a distasteful marriage, and followed you because of our friendship. I told him you'd tried to send me back to England and indeed, Harry, he behaved both sensibly and kindly. I don't like him much, I think he's a coxcomb and a libertine, but one must be just! He said I might continue the masquerade, but that when the battle is over, he will see I find a respectable situation. There!"

"You don't like him? You should kiss his boots for this," Harry said, his eyes glowing. "Oh, he's a capital fellow! As for being a libertine, stuff and nonsense! He's not a *monk*, certainly, but he's no rake, either. He doesn't need to be, for women like him, and he's confounded eligible. And he says he'll make all respectable, eh? Well he can, of course, for he knows all the best people, does Dan." He blew out his cheeks, exhaling on a long whistle. "That's a load off my mind, I promise you, Babs!"

"And off mine," Barbara agreed fervently. "Are you still beset with qualms about taking me in the advance party, to spy on the French army?"

"None, of course, if Dan thinks it right," Harry said, and presently Toby joined them, querulous because Barbara was going off with the officers, but not unhappy to remain in a billet where the food was good and Madame Guerin, the farmer's wife, determined to spoil him half to death.

" 'Morning, Lieutenant, 'morning, Bob," he said. "Do you want to 'ave a loan of me chive?" He flourished a wicked-looking blade under Barbara's nose, grinning as she put out a cautious finger to test its edge. "Careful, cully, it's sharp! You could despatch a Frenchman wiv one good thrust!"

He jabbed theatrically at empty air, one arm outflung, as though he held a duelling sword and not the rather sinister-looking knife.

"Thanks, Toby," Barbara said, taking the knife and sticking it into her belt. "Though I don't suppose I shall dig it into anything more exciting than a cheese; unless it's a ham!"

"You never know," Toby said darkly. "If there ain't no action, why ain't the officers wearin' uniform?"

"We could scarcely nip over the border into France and wander through French villages in rifle green! Come to that, if I wandered into a French village and stuck a knife into a local peasant, it might occasion remark!"

Toby sniggered, but insisted that she might have reason yet to be grateful for his timely loan.

"You may be right," Barbara said diplomatically. She began to lead her pony out of the stable in the wake of Harry, who had listened with a curling lip to Toby's animated conversation. "Goodbye for now, Toby. I'll see you in a few days."

"Goo'bye," Toby said gruffly. "Good luck!"

At the gate, Barbara turned to wave, but Toby had already disappeared back into the stables.

She was the last of their small company. Hurrying the pony, Moll, along the road, she contemplated the backs of her companions as she gradually drew closer. There was Captain Alleyn, riding Snowcloud. He sat the mare easily, almost slouching in the saddle, his worn clothing blending with the landscape; his saddlebags packed, a net of hay hanging from his stirrup leather. Then there were the two lieutenants; her own Harry, riding straight-backed, his blue coat, drab leather breeches, and long boots making him seem the leader of the party, whilst George, mountainous and at ease in an earth-coloured coat and dun-coloured breeches, sat Hannibal in a style almost as relaxed as the Captain's. The remaining rider was Sergeant Tallow and he, Barbara knew, had been included in the party on two counts; he had a good command of French, having been captured and imprisoned for several months in the Peninsular campaigns, and he was one of the best shots in the regiment; a sniper, Captain Alleyn had called him.

Harry, whose grandmother on his mother's side had been a Frenchwoman, an *aristo* who had fled in the days of the revolution, was needed for his excellent, idiomatic French. She knew that Daniel would lead and plan their moves, of course, and that George was a first-rate second-in-command, and supposed she herself had been included to add a touch of realism to the party. A lad who could wander around French villages unremarked, with sufficient grasp of the language to answer simple questions, might be invaluable.

Presently Daniel turned in his saddle and called Barbara and the sergeant to gather round himself and the two subalterns.

"We're within fifteen miles of the border into France," he began. "And probably no more than twenty miles from the French army, therefore it behoves us to be careful. We must also remember that however friendly the French and Belgian villagers may seem, many of them have fought, in the past, for Boney. So don't talk too freely, and obey orders at all times. I command, with George as my deputy." He paused, eyeing them thoughtfully. "You must understand that in enemy territory, it is experience which counts. Therefore, should George and myself be . . . elsewhere, you must turn to Sergeant Tallow for orders. Is that clear?"

"Yes, sir," Barbara said at once and heard Harry mutter discontentedly before, under Daniel's hard gaze, he reddened, saying, "Well, I *am* an officer, after all! But I'll do as you say, Dan, of course."

"And as Sergeant Tallow says, should the occasion arise?"

"That's what I meant," Harry said. "And I suppose if the sergeant should be absent as well, you'll rely upon Bob here to see me safe home?"

Daniel grinned. "I think in the event of myself, George and Tallow being hors de combat, you might safely consider yourself in command."

Harry grinned back. "Oh, well perhaps you're right, the sergeant has got the experience. But by the time we return to our billet, I shall be a lot less green!"

"I hope so." Daniel clicked to Snowcloud and they began to move down the road once more. "We must press on, now. I want to bivouac tonight just on the border. Then we can begin operations first thing tomorrow."

They made their camp in a small wood, and Barbara was torn between a strange, subdued feeling that the very trees had ears and might be enemy agents, and an enormous elation that she was doing something, at last, to help her country.

They had carried with them one small tent but the night was fine, so they arranged their sleeping blankets round the last dull glow of the campfire and rolled into them; save for Sergeant Tallow, who was to take the first watch.

Barbara lay awake for a little, gazing up through the branches overhead, at the stars which twinkled so brightly in the night sky. Then, almost without her knowing, her lids drooped over her eyes and she slept.

She woke, briefly, when Tallow struggled into his blanket and Harry took over the watch; she saw him cautiously push another crackling-dry branch into the glowing embers and then get to his feet and pad softly to the edge of the thicket. Then she slept again.

Rain falling lightly on to her upturned face awoke her.

For a moment she could not at all understand what was happening and obeyed her first impulse, which was to snuggle deeper into the blanket. Then she remembered and sat up, knuckling her reluctant eyes, which had no desire to do their duty by her and tell her what was happening in the encampment.

Looking round, she saw George come quietly over and crouch by Daniel. He breathed the other's name and Daniel was instantly awake and alert, but George merely said in a low voice, "The confounded rain threatened to put the fire out, so I covered it. We're protected from the worst here, however, and I think it won't last long. Shall I wake the others?"

"Yes, I think so. Then we can build up the fire and have a hot breakfast before moving out of here."

"Good. I kept some fuel dry, and once the kettle's on it will soon heat up."

Barbara sat up and ran her hands through her rumpled curls, then fished out her jacket and cloak, which she had lain on. Reflecting with satisfaction that though they might be creased, at least she would start the day dry and warm, she dressed, watching Sergeant Tallow woken, as the Captain had been, by a word. He in his turn woke Harry, who showed a tendency, in the first confused moments of waking, to curl up dormouse-like and ignore the call of duty.

But presently they were all up and eating a kind of porridge whilst Daniel was telling her to pour hot coffee into the mugs, and "Look lively, Bob!"

As she poured, the Captain spread a map out on the ground.

"We're . . . here," Daniel said judiciously, after a moment. "There's a village a few miles up the track." He measured the distance, then announced, "About two miles away, I'd think. Now, for our plan of campaign. Today we'll make contact with the people, find out where the army is at present. Harry, you and Bob can go ahead into the village and see what you can discover." He reached into his pocket and there was the clink of money changing hands. "Go into a bakery and buy bread, or into a shop of some description and buy something. Tell them you want to join the army. There are a thousand ways to win a peasant's confidence, and I'm sure you know them all. Then ride straight on through the village."

He paused, gazing at the map. "See, the road goes here, and tracks lead off, there and there." He frowned, whistling softly between his teeth. Suddenly his finger landed firmly on the paper. "That's it! See the wood a couple of miles outside the village? We'll meet there, at noon. We shall ride straight through the village without stopping and rendezvous with you on the outskirts of the wood. Is that clear?"

It was, and within a short time Harry and Barbara

were riding, side by side, down the narrow country road into the village.

Because of the rain the main street was deserted. Stone built cottages flanked the road, thatched and separated from the cobbles by a stream which ran perhaps four feet lower than their front gardens. Each cottage had a bridge of tree-trunks across the stream so that the occupants could cross dry-shod. There was also a blacksmith's forge, with a fire which billowed smoke, a wheelwright's establishment, an attractive little inn and, to their joy, a small bakery.

"I'll dismount and you may hold the horses," Harry said in a whisper. "You're my brother – *frère* – if anyone asks. I'll go in and buy some buns and some bread for the Captain, and see what I can find out. You wait here."

Before Barbara could say that she had no intention of being left behind, Harry swung off his horse, fired a positive volley of rapid French in her direction, and strode into the bakery, banging his head on the low doorway and uttering an anguished yelp which made Barbara hope that such involuntary exclamations were common to both French and English wounded!

Looking round through the thin rain, she saw a post and rail by the shop, plainly meant for horses, so she led their mounts over to it, looped their reins securely, and then wandered into the bakery.

Harry, listening to the baker who was apparently extolling the qualities of his long loaves of bread, turned and scowled at Barbara.

94

"*Méchant gosse*," he said. "*Ne t'ai-je pas dit d'attendre avec les chevaux?*"

Barbara, understanding this to mean that she had been told to remain with the horses, said sulkily, "*Oui, mon frère, mais . . .*"

The baker, turning to her, said kindly, "*Dehors, ce n'est pas très gai dans la place! Tiens, voici une brioche sucrée!*"

He handed her a sugared bun and Barbara, through a delicious mouthful, which, she hoped, would disguise any faults in her accent, agreed that it was dull in the square outside and thanked the man for his gift.

"*Oú vas-tu?*" The baker asked. "*Rejoindre l'armée?*"

Harry said that they were indeed hoping to join the army, and asked if they had much further to travel.

"*Non, non,*" the baker assured them. "*Peut-être à quatre ou cinq kilomètres.*" He went on to explain that the distance could not be more than a couple of miles or so since the soldiers came into the village regularly to have their horses shod and to obtain his excellent bread.

After mutual compliments, therefore, Harry and Barbara left the shop with some buns and the long French baguettes, which they pushed into their saddlebags before riding out of the village.

"Well, we've found out everything Dan wanted to know, I think," Harry said as they made their way towards the wood where they were to meet. "In fact Babs, I did very well! Especially since you might well have ruined everything, trotting in like that. My heart was in my mouth, I can tell you!"

"I thought you might have been stunned by that blow on the head, and forget your French," Barbara said demurely, glancing at him from under her lashes. "What a wallop it was, Harry! You must have been tempted to swear!"

Harry grinned. "I'm just glad you weren't near enough to hear what I *did* say when I staggered into the wretched shop! The baker, fortunately, seemed to expect no less. He said many choice phrases have been culled from the victims of his low doorway."

"Oh, I heard, but my French isn't good enough to understand," Barbara said regretfully. "Never mind, Harry, you must teach me some of those words. They sounded magnificent. What does *'merde'* mean?"

"Ah! Well, a rough translation would be curse it," Harry said cautiously. "Don't you go using words like that though, Babs, or you'll give people the impression that you're a nasty brat like Toby!"

"Toby's all right," Barbara said. "You only dislike him because you think he stole your silver-backed hairbrushes!"

"Think? He did!"

"That isn't the point, Harry. The point is that you thought it! Or that's what Toby says, at any rate."

"Yes, that sounds like Toby's logic," Harry said, with a reluctant laugh. "Thank the Lord he's not with us, though. That imp of Satan would probably steal the French *colours*, and try to sell them back to the Emperor!"

"Would that be a bad thing?"

Harry laughed again. "Only if he were caught! But come to think of it, that might be best all round. Many's the time I've longed to put Toby against a wall and shoot him myself!" They were in the shadow of the first trees now and he reined in his horse. "Better get into the wood a little way, where we can see without being seen. Then we'll hail them as they ride by."

"I hope we don't have long to wait," Barbara said, as the horses stood uneasily beneath the dripping branches. "It's horribly clammy and cold here."

Fortunately the rest of their little band were barely ten minutes behind them, and presently they were all pressing further up the road.

"You've done well," Captain Alleyn said when he had heard their story. "So the French army is just ahead of us, eh? Well I think for a start, we'll try for some details which the Duke will want; numbers, equipment and so on. We'll make our way nearer their encampment, then we'll split up. You and I, George, will try to infiltrate the enemy ranks as unobtrusively as possible." He surveyed Harry and Barbara thoughtfully. "Yes, you've both done your share. You and the Sergeant may wait for us at some convenient place which I'll point out when I see how the land lies."

They rode on, into an afternoon which was already brightening. The rain had stopped and gentle sunshine was making the countryside beautiful. Birds were singing and nearby they could hear a stream, chattering sweetly over the stones in its path. Presently they came to a small, hump-backed bridge and as they crossed it Barbara, glancing to her right, saw a youth of about Toby's age, watering three cavalry chargers.

Clearly, so that the others should hear, she said, *"Bonjour, mon ami! Que faites-vous?"*

Before the boy had a chance to point out that any fool could see he was watering horses, Daniel had called an interrogation as to the whereabouts of the army, and received a *"C'est là, m'sieur,"* in a shrill voice from the lad.

Following his pointing finger, they could soon make out for themselves the first sight of the army, only a couple of fields away. Thanking the boy, they rode forward.

"There's a barn ahead," Captain Alleyn remarked presently. "Largeish, by the look of it, and still in the shelter of the trees. We'll make sure it's empty and then we'll leave the horses there. You three," nodding to the Sergeant, Harry and Barbara, "may make yourselves comfortable until our return, which won't be long delayed. I doubt we'll be gone more than an hour. And then we'll move back, probably into the shelter of the woods again, before bivouacking for the night."

The barn, when they reached it, proved to be both empty and reasonably secure. The big door, latched with a wooden bar across it from the outside, meant that their horses could not roam off and Barbara, spying a ladder, climbed up and announced that the hayloft commanded a good view of the surrounding countryside, including a bird's-eye view of the

French army, which seemed to be spread out over a considerable part of the ground ahead of them.

"I expect it's a division or two out on manoeuvres," Daniel said. "But once we're there, we can tell from the uniforms which regiments are represented, and can count the artillery and the cavalry and so on. We'll just get changed, I think. Peasants are unremarkable enough in this landscape, goodness knows. You three wait for us here."

Daniel and George donned capacious blue smocks and changed their riding boots for ancient and cracked footwear such as the peasants wore, and then climbed down from the hayloft and rejoined the others by the horses.

"If we're gone for more than an hour," Daniel said, "you'd best make your way back to the woods. Carefully, mind. But leave our mounts here unless you're discovered, because if they suspect us and hold us we're bound to escape soon enough, and we shall need our horses to get us back to Belgium."

"Yoooir," Sergeant Tallow said, saluting, but the Captain said easily, "None of that, man! We're only a couple of peasants! Goodbye for now."

The two officers slouched out, grinning as they slipped round the big door, and dropped the wooden bar into place.

"Hey, can we get out?" Harry said, alarmed.

"Yes; there's a big gap between the door and the frame," Sergeant Tallow said. "See?"

He lifted the wooden bar to prove his point, then dropped it back into its socket.

"Let's watch them," Barbara said. She raced up

into the hayloft and the two men followed more slowly.

"And now to be bored for an hour," Harry said, throwing himself down in the hay as their companions were lost to view amongst the French tents. He cocked an eye at the Sergeant. "Should we sleep, Tallow, while we wait?"

"Aye, a cat-nap's never a bad idea," the Sergeant said. "I'll wake in an hour and we'll watch for their return from the window."

Barbara saw the two men settle down and speedily fall asleep, but she felt wide awake. She perched herself up in the wide, glassless window and watched the army. It was comfortable sitting there in the full sunshine, and warm; she closed her eyes though she was not at all tired, and was astonished when the Sergeant sat up and said, "They coming back yet, nipper? An hour's past."

Blinking in the sun, she surveyed the landscape. "No, not yet. There's no sign of movement in the fields which separate us from the army."

Half an hour passed without a sign of Daniel or George. Harry slumbered, a picture of innocent contentment, but the Sergeant and Barbara grew increasingly anxious.

"I'm off to 'ave a look," Sergeant Tallow said at last. "You'd best wake Mr. Kimberley. If I'm not back in an hour, you scarper, do you understand? Clear out! Wait for us the night, in that wood outside the village, and if there's no sign of us by morning get back to Brussels with as much information as you can remember."

"Right," Barbara said. She shook Harry and saw the bewilderment in his blue eyes as they opened on the dusty sunshine and ancient rafters of the old barn.

"Take care, Sergeant," she whispered, peering down into the stable part of the barn below, where Tallow was creaking open the big old door.

He grinned and raised a hand to her, then he was gone and Barbara was explaining to a sleep-befuddled Harry that it was growing late in the afternoon, that the Captain and the Lieutenant had still not returned, and that the Sergeant had set off in search of them.

Harry got up and lounged over to the window, then sprawled in the hay beside Barbara, who was watching Sergeant Tallow's seemingly lazy and purposeless amble towards the army.

"They'll turn up," he said comfortably. "They've probably found it more difficult than they expected to get all the information they want. In my opinion, I should have gone. I could talk myself out of trouble much easier than they could."

"Yes, but you wouldn't recognise the things they think are important," Barbara pointed out. She knelt before the window, straining to see the distant encampment more clearly. "If only I could see them!"

Harry, looking up at her silhouetted against the sinking sun, said, "Good God!" He reached up and pulled her down so that she was in the hay beside him. "Do you know, when you're against the light like that I can *see* you're a girl!"

"You know I'm a girl," Barbara said impatiently. "Don't be silly!"

He put his arm round her shoulders, hugging her to him. "You know what I mean!" He squeezed her so hard that it hurt. "You're so soft and lovely!"

"Stop it!" Barbara said, trying to struggle free. "Don't be such a nodcock, Harry, when the others may be in danger."

But he pulled her down, then leaned up on his elbow and gazed into her face. She noticed, with a little stab of fear, that his nostrils were flared, his mouth trembling strangely.

"You're safe here, with me," he said thickly. "And we're alone. Alone, Babs!"

She rolled out from under his arm but he pinned her against the side of the barn, holding her so close that she could scarcely move. She felt his mouth, loose and soft, fasten on her lips and she gave a choked little cry, fighting her arms free so that she might push against his chest.

He loosened his hold, saying sulkily, "What's the matter, Babs? Don't you want to be kissed? Damn it, aren't I allowed to kiss the girl I'm going to marry?"

He looked outraged and hurt and Barbara said, her voice shaking, "No! It . . . it isn't right, Harry, not now! And you held me so tight, and . . ."

He was watching her lips, his eyes glittering, and then he was on her again, saying, "Babs, my own love! We're good as betrothed, remember. You must allow me . . ."

She felt his hands hot on her small breasts as he

fumbled with her shirt fastenings. Panic tore at her. This was not Harry, her childhood friend! This was someone altogether different, someone with a loose-lipped, lustful mouth, hands which probed and squeezed, and a thick, strange voice which muttered of her duty to allow him more liberty now that they were almost betrothed.

She tried to push him away but he was strong, and his claims to more intimate caresses sounded so self-righteous that she was confused. He pressed her against the wall, one arm imprisoning her whilst the other moved over her body. She felt seeking fingers wrench at her shirt front and even as she gasped, "No! No!" his hand, warm and damp, invaded her bare breast.

His touch galvanised her into action. Hatred, strong and satisfying, swamped the confusion which his words had wrought. Betrothed or not, he had no right to tumble her in the hay the first time they were alone, and to touch her like this!

She writhed in his grasp, bringing her knee up and kicking, at the same time dropping her head and biting the seeking hand. She heard him gasp, and then she was fighting him in earnest, kicking, punching, her arms free, whilst he protested weakly and backed away from her.

"No, no! I say, Babs, old girl! I say . . ."

She was glad to see that the glitter had faded from his eyes and that embarrassment seemed the prevalent emotion on his pink, perspiring face.

"Now!" She said breathlessly. She fastened her shirt with trembling hands, picked up her jacket and scrambled into it. "How dare you, Harry Kimberley?"

He was truly mortified, she could see that. He said, "Well, we're all but betrothed, and . . . you're so pretty, Babs! Hang it, why shouldn't I have a kiss? Did you have to fight like a wildcat? I wasn't trying to . . . well, you would have thought . . ."

"A *kiss*?" Her tone was withering. "That wasn't just a kiss. What would have happened if I'd not fought like a wildcat? Tell me that!"

"Nothing," Harry said defensively. "Nothing! I was just . . . just . . ."

Barbara swung away from him to face the window – and gave a cry of pleasure. "They're coming back! Thank God, they're safe and no one's hurt. At least, they seem safe and well."

Harry strode over and looked out. "Yes," he said absently. Then, on a stronger note, "Babs? I'm sorry, truly I am. I must have been mad!"

She turned and saw the old Harry, his eyes shining with nothing more than friendship, though his face sagged ludicrously with embarrassment.

She put out her hand and took his, patting it.

"I forgive you. But . . . Harry?"

He was grinning down at her, at ease with her once more.

"Yes, Babs?"

"I'm a *boy*, and we must neither of us forget it again until I'm back in my petticoats. Is that clear?"

"Of course! You're quite right, Babs . . . Bob, I mean. Don't worry. It was just the . . . the hay, the sunshine . . . being alone, even. It's all right, truly. I'm over it now."

"You make it sound like an attack of measles," Barbara said, grimacing. "Do I have your word, Harry?"

He grinned sheepishly, nodding. "Here's my hand on it."

They were shaking hands when below them, they heard the big door creak open and the three men enter the barn.

Barbara went to go towards the ladder but Harry's hand on her arm detained her. She turned, brows raised.

"You won't say anything to the Captain, Babs?"

She giggled. "Of course not! You're mad, Harry. It's forgotten."

He grinned too, his eyes losing their anxious look. "Come on then, let's find out why they were so long."

CHAPTER
SEVEN

As they prepared their meal that evening, the wanderers told their story.

"We were moving slowly round the outskirts of the camp, making a mental note of numbers and cannon and so on," George said ruefully, "when we were hailed by three men, trying to skin a rabbit for a stew. I couldn't understand much of what they said, but I gathered they wanted some vegetables to add to the dish, and were demanding that we fetch them some. I acted the part of a fool of a farm labourer, gawping at them, which was pretty easy in the circumstances, and then Dan turned and said '*pommes de terre*', and even I, with my limited knowledge of French, knew that meant potatoes, so I mumbled, '*Oui, oui, m'sieurs*,' and ambled off. I'd seen some turnips when we crossed the fields earlier, so I dug some out, which wasn't easy, and then took them back. Dan had skinned the rabbit by then and jointed it, and they were talking amongst themselves and occasionally ribbing him, or so I imagined. Then they began to play dice, and we tried to leave, but they kept shouting something at us and we were getting somewhat flummoxed – or at least, I was – and then Tallow came up."

"I was never more thankful to see a man," Daniel said, grinning at the Sergeant. "I couldn't make out much of what that ugly-looking customer was saying, he was speaking French with the thickest and most abominable accent, but Tallow stormed at us, calling us idle beasts very likely, and worse, and proceeded to march us off, very crestfallen." He grinned at Harry and Barbara, who were listening open-mouthed. "It was a nasty moment when they kept insisting that we mustn't leave and I couldn't for the life of me make out why."

"They wanted to play you at cards, I think, sir," Sergeant Tallow said diffidently. "The trouble was, the fellow with the pack of cards had gone off somewhere. They asked if you'd got any pretty little sisters who might like to entertain them, and when you didn't rise to the bait, they changed their ploy to a bargain – they would contribute a few sous each, and would play against a plump young chicken for their pot. They thought you were farmers of some sort, you see."

"Oh, was that it?" Daniel said, grinning at George. "When he kept on about '*Un jeune poulet potelé*', I thought he was trying to get off with George, here!"

"No, sir. It means a plump young chicken, but it is used to describe a pretty young girl as well. Much as you might say a pretty little ladybird when in fact you're not referring to an insect at all!"

"A lesson in morals as well as French," Harry said, whilst George fell on Daniel.

The Captain, parrying the attack with a grin, said,

"Less of that, Georgie; you shouldn't have such a pink-and-white complexion. No, no, I take it back, don't steamroller me, you fool, I'm your superior officer!"

The two drew apart, grinning and apparently none the worse for having behaved like schoolboys for ten minutes. Daniel, brushing moss off his shabby breeches, said briskly, "Dish up that stew in about ten minutes, will you, George? I'm going to collect some dry fuel so that we can keep the fire in tonight. Bob, you come with me. The rest of you, get the camp set out ready for the night and see that the nags are tethered. I don't want them breaking away and cantering off when we're trying to get a decent sleep."

Barbara got to her feet and followed the Captain into the wood. When they were some way from the camp Daniel stopped, and caught hold of her shoulders, turning her to face him.

"Well? What happened this afternoon to make young Harry so stiff and awkward when we came back? And you so breathless and pink? I told that fool Tallow to stay with you, but I could scarcely say why! I suppose young Kimberley took advantage of your situation and kissed you?"

Barbara felt a tide of crimson engulf her. She hung her head.

"Am I right?"

Still with lowered eyes, she nodded.

Captain Alleyn caught her chin and tilted it until she had to meet his eyes. "Foolish creature! Harry's young and impulsive. He meant no harm, I'm sure;

it was the action of an eager stripling, rather than the advances of a libertine." He laughed, his eyes slitting with amusement. "No one knows better than I how seriously you take a kiss! Don't let it upset you, my child, but remember another time not to be alone with a man who knows your secret. Now brace up! I'll guarantee that if you're careful, the situation won't arise again."

A little smile curled Barbara's lips. "I'm alone with you now!"

He smiled back, rather grimly, she thought. "And as safe as if you really were a lad. I don't trifle with little girls, and to take advantage of your disguise would be a dirty trick."

Stung by his reference to "little girls", she said sharply, "You took advantage of Miss Barbara Campion, Captain Alleyn."

He laughed again. "That still rankles, doesn't it? To kiss a pretty girl when one has had a few glasses of champagne, and has just danced with her by moonlight, is no sin! But as I've said, you're safe from me now."

Barbara bent and picked up a branch of dry wood, trying to ignore a vague feeling of disappointment which had been aroused by his words. So he had been drunk that memorable evening on the terrace!

"Good," she said. "You won't say anything to Harry though, will you? He was dreadfully ashamed afterwards, and as you say, a kiss means nothing."

He frowned. "I said nothing of the sort! In fact . . . but this is neither the time nor the place for my views on kissing! If you think Harry will behave himself in future . . ."

"Of *course* he will, Captain Alleyn," Barbara said, with unnecessary force. "He said we were almost betrothed, and . . ."

"If he's almost betrothed to anyone, it is to Barbara Campion, and not Bob Garland. Remind him of that, if you please. And *do* try not to be alone with just one man again!"

"I've already agreed to be careful," she pointed out, her voice cold.

"So you have."

They completed their task in silence, then turned back towards the camp.

"What shall we do tomorrow?" Harry said drowsily when, their meal eaten, they were lying in their blankets around the glowing fire.

Barbara, who was on the first watch, was squatting on her haunches, feeding the embers carefully with small pieces of stick. She said, "Is it our turn now, Captain Alleyn? Mine and the Lieutenant's, I mean. To go and speak to the French soldiers?"

"Not you, Bob. Tomorrow I want Harry and the Sergeant to go and mingle. Just get general information, more on the lines of morale, who will be fighting under whose command, what they think of their chances, and so on. They've got untried green-'uns, same as us, and allies who don't know one end of a musket from the other. Then when you've done that, we'll make our way back to Brussels."

Harry muttered, "Very good, Dan," and soon, they slept.

Barbara enjoyed her watch. She was wide awake, having spent a lazy afternoon in the hayloft until Harry's attentions had forced her into activity, and now she prowled softly round the clearing, watching the road from time to time, for it could be seen dimly through the trees. But the time passed without incident and soon she was waking Sergeant Tallow up and curling into her own blanket, to slumber soundly until morning.

In the end Barbara had accompanied Harry and the Sergeant and they returned to the wood at noon, flushed with success.

"Everyone treated us quite naturally," Barbara said, in high spirits. "It was a good idea of mine, Captain Alleyn, to sell those sugar buns so cheaply. My basket was empty in no time, and they told me to come back tomorrow and bring twice as many!"

"Then they won't be moving on tomorrow," George said. "What of their feelings for Boney, and their hopes of success?"

Harry pulled a face and flung himself down beside the fire. "They're full of confidence in the Emperor," he admitted. "To hear them talk you'd think 'L'Empereur' was some sort of a God, and not a mere mortal! They swear he's invincible and can only lead them to victory. Yet they have no faith whatsoever in their generals and other leaders; suspect poor old Ney, because they say a man who changes sides once can do so again, and talk darkly of treachery in their own ranks, spies everywhere, that sort of thing. Yet they believe in Napoleon, as though he alone could win the battle single-handed."

"Well, they'll find themselves mistaken when they meet us in the field," Daniel said grimly. "It's to our advantage if they put all their faith in Bonaparte, because he can't be everywhere at once. What of the rest? Did you find out anything else?"

"They seem to have odds on us in sheer numbers," Harry said. "But they're afraid of the English, Dan, really they are. They don't like our squares, or our artillery, and they say the men who fought in Spain are regular devils, because they won't line up neatly where they can be seen, but hide and ambush in an unmilitary but brilliantly effective way. That's what their veterans say, but of course, like us, they've a lot of Johnny Raws amongst 'em this time. Men who've not fought before. But I'd say the general feeling is one of confidence – because they believe Napoleon to be unbeatable."

"And you, Tallow?"

"Oh, I got much the same impression as the Lieutenant," Sergeant Tallow said. "Numbers will be crucial, I believe. But you'll want all that information writ down, when we're in Brussels."

Daniel nodded. "Yes, that would be best. And now we'd best start our journey back." He had been scattering the fire with great thoroughness and now he rose to his feet, dusting his hands. "Come along! Bob, you borrowed that basket from the baker, didn't you? Ride back to the village with it, there's a good lad, and take it back to the shop. We might need his friendship again one of these days. Do you want Harry to go with you?"

"No, I'll go ahead," Barbara said. "You'll want to pack up and clear away all signs of our camp and then you can catch me up." She chuckled, standing up to pat Mollie's neck. "My pony's not exactly the speediest thing on four legs!"

"Well, if you're sure. Off with you, then."

Barbara mounted the pony and Harry handed her the big, flat-bottomed basket. "Don't start chattering to the baker," he advised. "Just give him the basket – *le panier* – back. He'll ask you if the buns sold well, '*Est-ce qu'on à bien vendu les brioches?*', and you say 'Yes, a thousand thanks,' and ride on your way."

"I'm not helpless, you know," Barbara said. "Goodbye!"

It was a fine afternoon, the sun shining brightly through the green of the summer foliage overhead. Barbara rode into the village, crossing the stream by the hump-backed bridge, singing a little French song she had heard in the camp. It was in a happy frame of mind that she rode across the square, with no premonition of trouble ahead.

She looped Mollie's reins round the tethering post and ducked through the low doorway into the bakery. The shop was not empty, for a tall, heavily built soldier stood there, leaning against the counter. He wore the green coat, faced with white, and the scarlet plumed helmet of a French dragoon and as Barbara entered the shop, basket on arm, he swung round and stared at her.

"*Votre panier, monsieur, et merci beaucoup, beaucoup,*" Barbara gabbled, pushing the basket across the counter towards the baker. *"Bonjour, messieurs."*

She was halfway to the door when the dragoon roared out, *"Arrête-toi! Où vas-tu?"*

Barbara remembered telling the baker on her first visit that Harry was her brother. *"Chez mon frère, Monsieur le Capitaine,"* she said desperately. *"Mon frère est soldat."*

The dragoon smiled, apparently well content to hear that her brother was a soldier. *"Alors, tu peux monter à cheval avec moi et remporter ton panier, mais cette fois-ci, rempli de pain pour le mess des soldats."*

Barbara's mind whirled. If she did as the dragoon asked and returned to the camp with him, they might meet Daniel and the others. If so, what disaster might occur! They might hail her in English, or . . .

"Mais non, monsieur, s'il vous plaît," she said, *"Je dois m'en aller maintenant."*

The dragoon obviously did not relish being told that she could not wait for him. *"Non, attends-moi, gamin!"* he said sharply.

He obviously took her compliance for granted, turning to the baker and telling him imperiously to load his loaves into the "gamin's" basket.

The baker looked uneasy; Barbara realised he had not been paid and saw small chance of ever seeing his money, for the French army requisitioned its supplies remorselessly – a fact which did not endear it to any of the peasants through whose territory it passed.

Whilst he hesitated, the dragoon began to put the loaves into the basket himself and Barbara, seeing her chance, turned and dashed out of the shop. She whipped the reins free from the tethering post, vaulted into Mollie's saddle, and crouching forward on the pony's neck, urged her to a gallop.

The dragoon, burdened with the bread and the unwieldy basket, erupted from the shop, shouting. *"Reviens, reviens, misèrable! Quel toupet . . . de désobéir aux ordres . . ."* She relaxed a little. He might shout at her, but at least it seemed he did not mean to pursue her. And then she heard his voice rise urgently. *"Déserteur! Espion! Attrapez-le! Après lui!"*

That's torn it, she thought, bending low over Mollie's neck once more. He had sent someone in pursuit, with injunctions to follow and catch him. Yes, she could hear horses' hooves clattering over the cobbled square. She dared a glance over her shoulder and saw figures on horseback not far behind. Mollie thundered up the narrow lane, with the wind now tearing the sounds of pursuit away, but she knew they were getting closer.

Out of the corner of her eye she saw a horse's nose just level with Mollie's tail. She swerved and the horse squealed, someone shouted, and then she was flying through the air, the lane, the sky, the hedgerow whirling giddily round her. She felt the yielding impact of the hedge, then something hard hit her across the head and she knew no more.

She came round to find herself lying face downwards across the withers of a white horse. She saw the dust of the lane stirred up by its hooves and felt the smooth movements of the well-muscled shoulders as it strode onwards. She moved, giving a small groan, for she was stiff and aching, but the movement started her slipping towards the ground and she braced herself for the fall.

A hand caught hold of the waistband of her breeches, however, stopping her descent, and a voice said reassuringly, "Steady, steady! You're safe. Can you sit up?"

She would have known that voice anywhere. "Captain Alleyn! What on earth. . . . Where are the French? I thought they'd got me, they were so close, and when I swerved, and . . ."

"You mean Mollie swerved and you kept straight on," Daniel said. "I've never seen a flying stableboy until today, but you took to the air like a bird! Good thing the hedge stopped you, or you'd have sailed on for another dozen yards or so, like one of Whinyate's rockets!"

He slowed Snowcloud, put his hands round Barbara's waist, and lifted her into a sitting position. Barbara found herself swaying before him, sick and giddy, but all in one piece.

"I . . . I don't understand," she stammered, looking about her. Nearby, George smiled reassuringly at her from Hannibal's broad back and Harry sat Taffy, and behind them Sergeant Tallow rode his bay gelding and led Mollie.

"It was us," Daniel said patiently. "That dragoon – what *had* you done to him? – burst out of the bakery shouting the equivalent of thief, robber and get after him, and since we were the only people in sight, naturally we set off in hot pursuit. Only as soon as we were safely out of the hearing of the dragoon, we tried to call you. And did you take any notice? Devil a bit! Then, when Harry managed to put a spurt on and brought Taffy right up close, you swerved across his path, Mollie stumbled, and you flew through the air. He's a good rider, and managed to save his own seat." He grinned down at her. "I take it you thought we were avenging Frenchmen?"

"Well, naturally," Barbara said with dignity. "And now, sir, I'll mount my own pony, if you please. I'm sure Snowcloud would sooner carry a single burden than a double."

"As you please," he said indifferently. "Are you able to sit your mount, though? We don't want you fainting on us."

"I shan't," Barbara said. He obligingly drew Snowcloud to a halt and she slipped down, walked back and mounted Mollie, feeling that she had made a complete fool of herself.

After riding silently beside the Sergeant for ten minutes, Barbara risked a quick glance at his countenance. He grinned encouragingly, and she said, "You must think me addlepated! I was so *sure* you were the enemy!"

"You did well," Tallow said. "The way you made Mollie jink across the lane was excellent strategy. And anyone can be thrown when the horse stumbles."

Harry, dropping back, said curiously, "What happened in the bakery, Bob? You certainly did seem to annoy that dragoon! His face was as scarlet as his helmet plume!"

"He told me to carry bread back to the French officers' mess," Barbara explained. "But I dared not obey him in case I either missed you, or you met me and called out. I was lucky really, because when he ordered the baker to put the loaves in the basket, the baker didn't. I think he knew he'd not be paid. The dragoon started to load the basket himself and I turned and ran, and I suppose he couldn't run after me with the bread, but wouldn't leave it in case the baker changed his mind and took it back."

"And then we rode in, like avenging angels, and he shrieked at us to follow you. Well, I hope he isn't still standing in the middle of the village square, waiting for us to return!"

"I hope he is," Barbara said vengefully. "I hope he waits for ages and gets into trouble from his officers, horrible man!"

Harry laughed but made no further comment, and they continued on their way, growing more confident with every mile which they put between themselves and the French army.

Late that night they rode into their billet once more. Barbara was so tired that she was swaying in the saddle, but there was to be no respite.

"Right, Bob, get to work on the horses," Captain Alleyn said peremptorily. "You'll find a meal in the kitchen when you've done. Roust Toby out and get him to give you a hand."

"I'll be too tired to eat," Barbara said, leading Mollie into the end stall and beginning to undo her girths.

George, unsaddling Hannibal, said comfortingly,

"Never mind, Bob, we shall all take the gear off our own mounts and rub them down. All you'll have to do when you've finished Mollie is feed and water 'em."

"All! I wish someone would feed and water me!" She raised her voice to a shout. "Hi, Toby, you lazy toad! Come down and give me a hand."

Silence answered her.

Harry, wearily unsaddling Taffy, said, "I'll get the little brute," and climbed into the loft and presently an outraged yelp, followed by whining complaints, proved that Toby had indeed been up in the loft, with no intention whatsoever of lending a hand.

Driven down the ladder, however, and into the lamplit stable, he knuckled his eyes, peered at Barbara, and then said resignedly, "Awright, awright, awright, I'll give you a 'and with them prads! Fair's fair, and I've 'ad a restful couple of days of it." He turned to glare malevolently at Harry. "I've not missed Lieutenant Pretty-boy, though, 'cept for the better, like."

"You cheeky varmint," Harry began wrathfully, but Daniel said, "Stubble it, Harry, we're all tired out. Let's get these horses seen to, and then we can eat and have a few hours' sleep before we ride into Brussels tomorrow to report to the Duke."

Barbara, lugging a wooden bucket full of water across the stable, nearly dropped it. "The Duke? The Duke of Wellington? Oh, shall I go with you?"

"No," Daniel said shortly. He finished grooming Snowcloud and smoothed her velvet muzzle. "Good girl, then."

Barbara set the bucket of water down and Snow-cloud bent her head to drink.

"Why not?" Barbara said, outraged. "I've never seen the Duke! Oh, I do want to see him! I helped, you know I did. Why can I not go into Brussels to report?"

"Because the Duke would not want a stableboy's opinion," Daniel said icily. "Try for some sense, Bob." He turned to the other men. "Are you ready?"

As the men left the stable Harry lingered for a moment. He whispered, "Never mind, Babs; even if you don't go to see the Duke there's nothing to stop you from coming to watch over the horses while we go inside his hotel! And the chances are you'll see him, even if you don't speak to him."

Barbara said, in her small, gruff voice, "It doesn't matter, Lieutenant," and saw him linger, irresolute.

"You're not still cross – about that business in the barn?" he muttered at last.

Barbara humped the last bucket of water across to the last horse, stood it down, wiped the back of her hand across her forehead and said resignedly, "No, I've forgotten it. I shan't be long now."

Harry muttered, "Good, good," and strode off towards the farm kitchen.

Toby, mixing bran mash, said nobly, "I'll finish off 'ere, Bob. You go an' get yourself some prog."

"I'm too tired to be hungry," Barbara said wearily. "If you mean it though, Toby, I'll go up to the loft." She yawned prodigiously, rubbing her eyes. "Gawd, I'm wore out," she said, in faithful imitation of Toby himself. "Goodnight."

She climbed the ladder in a daze, and almost fell into her blanket. But not to sleep. Tired though she was her mind was active, going over and over the episode with Harry in the barn, and Daniel's subsequent lecture. It had been hateful of Harry to attack her like that. Hateful but, she supposed, understandable. And Daniel had been worse! To say he had only kissed her because he was a trifle drunk was bad enough, but then to go on in that superior fashion about not trifling with 'little girls', and insinuating that Harry had done so . . .

Well, it was enough to drive all thoughts of sleep out of her head!

She lay there, growing more and more indignant. Harry thinks I'm pretty, she told herself. Why doesn't Daniel seem to notice? Not that she wanted him to! Indeed, if he had the temerity to so much as squeeze her hand she would have taught him a sharp lesson. But . . . but. . . .

Her thoughts began to slide into one another. Harry, the French dragoon with his scarlet-plumed helmet, the hooves of the chase, Daniel not kissing her, Harry kissing her so forcibly, Daniel not even *wanting* to kiss her . . .

Indignation was dispersed in weariness.

She slept.

CHAPTER
EIGHT

"It's too bad! I helped it get the information, didn't I, but now they've gone off into Brussels without me. They wouldn't even take me to hold the horses! They'll have all the fun, they'll see the Duke and all the other important people, and get praised for their work, and we shall just wait here!"

Barbara and Toby were tucking into one of madam's savoury stews and Toby, spearing a dumpling, said judiciously, "Yes, Bob, but after they've seen the Duke they're going to the Duchess of Richmond ball! Oh, I know they were only invited 'cos of the talk they 'eard at the French camp, but they couldn't take us along, could they? No use kicking against what can't be 'elped."

"No-oo," Barbara admitted. "Not inside, I grant you. But they could have taken us along to watch the fun."

"What fun? Not much fun watchin' a pack of flash morts rollin' their eyes at every officer in sight! No, I'd liefer be 'ere, I would."

"Why?" Barbara asked suspiciously. "It isn't like you to want to be left out of anything."

Toby looked shifty. "I've gotta game going. None of your business, Bob, but I don't reckon we'll be 'ere much longer, and. . . . Well, I'd liefer be 'ere this evening."

Barbara wiped her bread round her plate and said, "Delicious, madam," to the farmer's wife. The woman bustled forward, all smiles, to clear the table and Barbara told Toby, "I'm going to Brussels, then. I won't be stuck here all evening by myself."

"If we march at dawn, you'll regret it," Toby warned her.

Barbara snorted. "Dawn! Sometimes I think we'll be here for always! Anyway, I'll be back long before dawn. Where are the Richmonds staying, do you know?"

"Rue de la Blanchisserie," Toby said, with an accent which made Barbara wince.

"Right. I'm off. Even if I can only watch the swells going in, I shall at least *see* the important people. The Prince of Orange will be there, and the young Duke of Brunswick, and Lord Uxbridge, and a great many others. I just won't miss seeing them all."

"I know what you mean," Toby admitted. "Every bloomin' rifleman knows old Nosey, an' Picton, an' Colborne; but you've been stuck out 'ere."

So Barbara set off in the long June evening, riding Mollie, taking deep breaths of the warm, scented air. It was a good evening, she told herself. Too good to be stuck in the stables or hanging round the farmhouse. And besides, Toby was up to something; she had no desire to find herself up to her ears in his mischief! She knew, of course, that if Captain Alleyn found out she was in Brussels he would be very angry; he had told her bluntly that her last trip into town had been unwise.

"Brussels is full of English people, some of whom may know you," he had said. "What if you walk into someone who recognises you despite your disguise? Your reputation would suffer."

But now, riding along the quiet country road with Brussels glowing in the evening light across the valley, she could not think of that. She could only think of all the excitement, the important people, she would see in Brussels tonight.

She took Toby's advice and left Mollie in a field on the outskirts of the city, then walked in. She made her way quickly and with reasonable ease to the Rue de la Blanchisserie, and then stood close to the entrance with many other eager persons, watching the guests arrive. She had never seen such numbers of beautifully-dressed women nor such an abundance of colourfully-uniformed men.

As she made her way to the front of the crowd, someone cried, "Hey! You, boy, in the uniform jacket. Do you want to earn yourself a shilling or two? Then take this note round to Number Fourteen, Rue de l'Honnerie. It is for Lady Alicia Craven."

The young officer who had spoken thrust a piece of paper into Barbara's hand with some coins, and then gave her a push. "Go on, lad, there's no time to waste!"

On hearing the name of Alicia Craven, Barbara's heart had stood still for a moment. For before her marriage some six months previously, Alicia Thripton had been Barbara's dearest friend. The youngest and least significant member of a large family of girls and boys, harassed Lady Thripton had been only too happy for Alicia to play with "that poor little Landrake dependant," as she had called Barbara.

And then Lord Craven had walked into the Assembly rooms where at least five Thripton girls were enjoying the informal dances which took place there monthly. And he had met, proposed to, and married Alicia in a whirlwind courtship which lasted barely four weeks.

But Alicia here? Her husband was certainly not an army man, and Barbara remembered Suzannah Thripton saying spitefully that he was no young blade, but a man of mature years. Could it be her friend, her own dear Allie?

She was roused from her reverie by the officer saying patiently, "Are you not English? I thought . . ."

"Yes, I'm English," Barbara said quickly. "But where is the Rue de l'Honnerie, sir?"

"Oh, not far. See that turning down there? Go right the way along it, to the end, and the first turning on your left is the Rue de l'Honnerie. Is that clear?"

"Yessir, thank you," Barbara gabbled, touching her shako. She took the note firmly in her hand and set off at a trot.

At the door, her knock was answered by a manservant, who held out his hand for the note.

"No, I am to deliver it into Milady's hand myself," Barbara said in French, her tone dulcet but her expression determined. She could not help a little shudder at the thought of meeting anyone but her own dear Alicia, but she stood firm.

The man hesitated, but plainly, he could see no harm in admitting a slim little lad. He led the way across the hall and into a small salon with a fire burning on the hearth despite the warmth of the evening.

"Her ladyship will be with you presently," he said in very good English, and closed the door behind him.

Barbara, left alone, wondered at her own temerity. Suppose she was confronted by some huge, commanding old dowager? Or worse, by someone who knew her as Barbara Campion?

Her doubts were cut short by the entrance into the room of a plump young person with dusky curls, bright blue eyes, and a sparkling smile.

"Yes?" The young person said enquiringly. "I believe you have a note for me?"

"Yes, it's from some young blade I met in the Rue de la Blanchisserie, Allie," Barbara said in her own voice. "What a way for a married woman to behave, though! Clandestine notes . . ."

She was interrupted.

"Babs!" Alicia shrieked. "Darling Babs, what *are* you doing here? And dressed as a boy!" She rushed forward and enveloped her friend in a scented embrace. "You *terrible* girl! As for clandestine notes, no such thing! I'll warrant it's from my own darling Rupert, saying he won't be able to go to the ball." She broke the seal on the note and scanned it rapidly.

"Oh, yes, what a nuisance! But never mind, I'll go on my own, as he suggests. Now, Babs, tell me! Dear God, your *hair*! Mind you, it's very pretty in a brief sort of way, but . . ."

"Allie, I'm with the army," Barbara explained. "I'm not supposed to be in Brussels at all, but I do want to see the Duke, and all the other swells! The thing is I had to run away from the Landrakes'; there was no bearing it. I say, I suppose I couldn't come to the ball with you, could I? As your page or something?"

"Not as my page; people know I don't have one. But you shall go, Babs!"

Barbara frowned. "How? I don't want my officers to see me and send me home in disgrace."

Alicia chuckled. "They won't! Come up to my room now, while there are no servants about, and we'll turn you into a girl again! Just for this evening, you know. And you can tell me the whole story."

"A girl again? But but what about my hair?"

Preceding her briskly up the stairs, Alicia said, "Easy! I've got false ringlets – who hasn't – and with a nice broad piece of ribbon or a fillet of flowers, we can fasten them so that no one will know they aren't your natural hair."

They reached her bedroom, an elegant apartment with a pale carpet and pink silk window curtains. "Now, Babs, tell me how you come to be here, and why you're wearing breeches."

Barbara told her story, leaving out nothing.

"Lord Chacewater wants to marry you? Surely not, Babs! He's quite an old man, I believe. At least,

I know his son and he's several years older than I am, probably thirty or thirty-five."

"He does want to marry me," Barbara insisted. "And you know what my uncle Landrake is like, Allie! So I ran away from home, and came to Harry."

Alicia, spreading out a variety of evening gowns on the bed, pursed her lips thoughtfully. "Harry? Of course, you used to adore him, didn't you? He was always great fun, but I can't imagine him taking care of you – or anyone, for that matter! Do I wrong him? Is he planning to marry you when the battle's over, and he can whisk you home to his mamma?"

"Well, he might, if all can be made respectable," Barbara said. "To own the truth, Allie, I've been rather taken aback to find that Harry. . . . well, he *said* he wanted to marry me, but . . ."

"Harry isn't very steady, or reliable," Alicia said. "My dear child, I should think everyone but yourself knew that! You were always his favourite because you were such a tomboy, and so game, and so ready to do as you were told. But you mustn't think he's going to take on the responsibility for a little wife who knows nothing of life and would be utterly dependent on him. He's too selfish, love!"

"Oh! But he said, in a few years . . ."

"Yes, because as he's well aware, in a few years he'll want to settle down. He'll have a house which he'll want a woman to run, and he'll want children and so on. But right here and now, a wife would just slow Harry Kimberley down!" She turned, a primrose gown over her arm. "This looks like you, my pretty Babs! Try it on!"

"I'd better wash first," Barbara said, looking from her sunburned arms to the delicate net and satin confection which Alicia was offering.

"Yes, perhaps you'd better," Alicia admitted, twinkling. "You look a real little gypsy, Babs. But just wait until I've finished with you. You won't know yourself!"

And half an hour later, Barbara, looking at herself in the mirror, felt that Alicia had not exaggerated. She had washed Barbara's cropped hair, then set the front in tiny formal kiss-curls across her forehead. The rest of her curls were allowed to dry naturally, but on top she had pinned the promised bunch of ringlets, the pins hidden by a band of primrose velvet ribbon. A faint dusting of face powder had made Barbara sneeze and protest, but it had filmed over her freckles, and the same powder, lightly dusted over her forearms, lightened the warm golden tan which the hot sunny days had given her.

And the gown! She blushed to see it, but Alicia was adamant.

"Yes, I *know* it shows your shape, and a very pretty shape you have to show! And I know it is cut low, but you don't want to look a *dowd*. No, I cannot lend you anything more missish, for two simple reasons. One is that I'm a married woman and have been these six months, so I've not got any plain muslins made high to the neck and long in the sleeve! And another is that I'm a tiny bit on the plump side, so when you put your maddeningly slim figure into my gowns, naturally they're a little bit loose for you on the top. See?"

"Yes, but do I look . . . noticeable?" Barbara asked urgently, as they made their way downstairs. "Not . . . not fast, or anything?"

Alicia laughed and squeezed her arm. "Of course not, my love! If you think I would encourage you to go to a ball in anything which was not perfectly proper, you wrong me! Indeed, you look so delightful that no one will notice me, and that will be annoying! Now, hold your head up high and *smile*!"

A carriage awaited them, the servants too well-trained to show any surprise over their mistress's new friend. Then they were climbing down outside the Richmonds' house, Barbara carefully holding up her borrowed petticoats so that she didn't tread them into the dust of the flagway, for Alicia being an inch or so taller, they were a little long for her.

"Come along, Babs dear," Alicia said gaily. She murmured to Barbara in an aside, "I simply must use your real name, dearest, for if you are to cast off this masquerade before you return to England, it may be remembered in your favour that you appeared at this ball with a respectable young matron chaperoning you. I'm very well known in Society, you know, thanks to my dear Rupert!"

"Yes, that's true," Barbara said, trying to remember to trip rather than stride, and to keep her glances demure instead of staring frankly into every face she encountered.

Once inside the house they were led straight into the ballroom, which had been transformed into an arbour of roses, colour, and brilliance. Pink silk draperies, rose-trellised wallpaper, and hangings of crimson, gold and black dazzled Barbara's eyes as much as the crystal chandeliers whose light streamed out of the open windows, turning the afterglow of evening into blue and gold. There were real roses too, vases, bowls, baskets of them. Their sweet scent seemed to swirl in the warm air as the music and the dancers themselves swirled.

"The Duke isn't here yet," Alicia remarked presently, as they sat themselves down on two little gilt chairs with pink silk seats. "But his latest flirt is. See the pretty woman over there? She's in blue, talking to that very tall man? She's Lady Frances Webster."

"She's also pregnant," Barbara observed frankly.

Alicia giggled. "Ssh! Yes, she is. But then they say the Duke's flirts are no more than that – he enjoys the company of women without wanting a sordid *affaire*."

"Well, she is very pretty . . ." Barbara was beginning, when a young man stood before them, bowing

"Lady Craven? I would very much like to be introduced to your young friend."

It was the beginning of a delightful interlude for Barbara. She was whisked into the dance and soon a variety of partners had stood up with her and indeed, had remained by her side to talk to her and the vivacious, delightful Lady Craven.

Once, in the press of people, Barbara saw Harry, and gave him an inviting smile, but his attention was upon a fluffy little blonde creature in a pink dress, and his glance flickered over her without recognition.

She saw Captain Alleyn, too, not dancing but

talking to a group of officers. They seemed to be sharing a serious conversation, for their voices were low, their expressions solemn.

Deliberately she moved across his line of vision and saw his glance rest on her without curiosity, and then people had moved between them and she could see him no longer.

Just after midnight, she danced with a tall and gangling young officer from the Fifteenth Light Dragoons, in the full glory of his blue, gold and red uniform, his short pelisse slung over one shoulder for the evening was very warm, despite all the windows being wide open to catch the slightest breeze.

"Miss Campion, the Duke's arrived. Have you met him? He's the gentleman standing over there, taking to Slender Billy – I mean the Prince of Orange."

Barbara stared with unabashed curiosity at the two men. The Prince of Orange was as slender as his nickname, a pale-skinned, nervous looking lad with light brown hair and an air of suppressed excitement. The Duke of Wellington was shorter than Barbara had expected, built wirily rather than imposingly, with a big, hooked nose, very dark hair and eyes, and a loud, rather abrupt laugh which suddenly rang round the ballroom, bringing everyone's attention to him. He seemed to realise this, for he beckoned to a pretty young girl standing nearby, seeming to recommend the Prince as a partner with another of his barks of laughter.

"That's Georgy Lennox," Barbara's partner informed her. "And the fellow the Duke's speaking to now, see him? is Lord Uxbridge, his second-in-command."

The dance ended, and Barbara's partner led her off the floor and over to where Alicia was standing, talking to her erstwhile partner.

"I think I'd best see if I can find my commanding officer," the young man said earnestly to Barbara. "Something's happening, by Jove! But th-thank you for a delightful dance, and I trust that we may soon meet again."

Presently, Barbara said to a young man who had been introduced to her as Captain Ealing, "Nothing has happened, then. I rather thought when the Duke came in and everyone buzzed so that all the officers would disappear! Are the rumours of an impending battle false, do you think?"

"False? No! But the Duke will see we're in the right place at the right time."

Barbara was reminded of her acquaintances in the French army, with their total trust in Napoleon to get them out of any scrape, and she could not but smile.

"I'm sure you're right," she said diplomatically. "And now, I think I'd best return to Lady Craven, for it is the supper dance next, I believe."

"Very well. I suppose you have a partner for supper?" And upon her agreeing that this was so, "I feared as much, for you are quite the prettiest girl I've met in Brussels."

Barbara, blushing a fiery red, was quite glad to be returned to Alicia's side once more.

"The trouble with you, my dear Babs, is that

you've never been into any sort of society, thanks to those mean, conceited Landrakes," Alicia said, on seeing her friend's rosy countenance. "Oh, I know you grew up with the Kimberleys, but they didn't treat you like a young lady, did they? Harry may have kissed you in the shrubbery and vowed his devotion, but that isn't like dancing with you and paying you pretty compliments! You were never even allowed to come to the Assemblies, and goodness knows, they were dull enough! When can you escape from your disguise? You see, Rupert and I may not be here much longer, and if possible I'd like you to return to England under our aegis. Truly, it would do very well, and I can think of some story to satisfy the curious."

"You are good, Allie, but I shall see it through to the finish," Barbara said gratefully. "I may well be glad to take advantage of your offer when the battle's over, if you're still here."

"I hope you know what you're doing," Alicia said. "You won't *fight*, will you Babs?"

"No, of course not. But they need me, Allie, to take care of the horses, and so on. I couldn't leave them now, when it's too late to replace me."

"No, I do see that. But take good care, Babs."

At this point, another gentleman approached and whisked Alicia off on his arm. Barbara surveyed the motley crowd before her, content to sit still for a moment. So many different uniforms, and such beautiful dresses. Glancing idly at the quantities of gold braid, the strange insignia of foreign brigades, she reflected that the room could have been infiltrated by a large number of spies from Napoleon's army, since not only could no one present have identified all the uniforms, but the whole house was open to the evening and people wandered in and out quite without ceremony.

It was at this point that she saw Daniel, in conversation with a General covered in gold braid, making in her direction. When they were within a few feet of her Daniel said to his companion, "If you will excuse me, your lordship, I will seek my partner now." The other nodded and made some joking reply and the two men parted, Daniel to come straight to her side.

"Miss Campion, will you honour me with your company for a few minutes?" he said, taking hold of her hand in a grip which could not be denied.

She began to protest, but he said grimly, "I insist!" and she realised that to struggle would be both undignified and fruitless.

"Where are we going?" She said breathlessly as he hurried her out of the ballroom. "I'm with a friend, you know, Lady Alicia Craven. She will wonder where I am!"

He did not reply, but led her to a small room which had been set aside for people wanting to talk rather than dance.

"Sit down," he said curtly. "Try to look as if I were flirting with you!"

"You could do so with perfect propriety," she said rather wistfully, "for I'm a young lady again, Captain Alleyn."

He ignored the coquetry in her tone. "The battalion will be on the move within the hour. We must both go back – unless you could stay here, with Lady Craven?"

She shook her head. "Impossible. Her husband has never met me, and besides my place is with the column."

He gave a short laugh. "You will be left in the rear, my child, with the rest of the baggage! I'll try to find you a safe billet, but I can't leave you with Madame Guerin, for we march out of Brussels in quite a different direction, to Braine le Compte in fact."

"Then I'd best get back to Alicia as quickly as can be, and tell her I must leave and put on my boy's clothes again." She hesitated, looking with unconscious pleading up into his face. "You're not annoyed with me?"

He sighed, then grinned. "I suppose you were desperate to find yourself in Harry's arms again, and you've done no harm by it. No, I'm not annoyed with you. In fact, if you can turn yourself back into a boy in . . ." he consulted his watch, "in twenty minutes, I'll ride back to the farm with you. Harry and George have already left. I spotted you and made an excuse to linger for a moment."

"Harry didn't recognise me, let alone dance with me," Barbara admitted. "And I'm sure I can be changed and ready to leave in twenty minutes."

He grinned at her again, with a look that kindled the warmth in her cheeks. "I'd know you anywhere." Before she could answer he was on his feet, bowing. "Will you have one last dance before you leave, Miss Campion?"

"Oh! Have we time?"

"It would look better than the pair of us leaving after a hurried conversation," he pointed out.

They made their way back to the ballroom, Barbara with her hand resting lightly on the Captain's arm. As they re-entered the room Alicia came towards them. "Babs, darling, I wondered where you were." She smiled dazzlingly at the Captain. "Daniel, don't say you're going to dance with my little friend! I thought you never danced!"

He smiled back. "Not never; but rarely. Come, Miss Campion."

It was a waltz and he danced better, if anything, than he had on the terrace. She felt that she could have danced for ever, though when he drew her so close she feared that he could even feel the fluttering of her heart. But he only said, looking down at her, "You have certainly chosen a pretty gown, Miss Campion! In fact, I've never seen my stableboy looking better!"

She twinkled up at him. "Just remember that when you're shouting at me to feed and water the horses, and to hurry up with the hay-nets," she reminded him.

His arm tightened round her waist. "Or when a terrible, eight-legged beast threatens to. . . . What was it threatening to do to you, my child?"

She shivered, laughing. "That's unfair, and it won't happen again, you know it won't."

They had circled the floor twice and now he led her towards Alicia, deep in conversation with a handsome, middle-aged gentleman.

He bowed profoundly to Alicia, then said to the

middle-aged gentleman, "My lord, is the Duke still here? I would like a word with him before I rejoin my brigade."

It was Barbara's cue. As the two men left them she said urgently to Alicia, "I've been ordered to leave at once! Captain Alleyn commands my company, and he will ride back to the farm where we're billeted with me, if I can be ready outside here in twenty minutes."

Alicia, always quick-witted, said, "Very well. I shall say you feel a little faint, because I must certainly return. Fortunately it isn't far to the Rue de l'Honnerie; we can walk there in five minutes, so we won't have to wait for the carriage to be brought round."

She hailed a gentleman in evening dress and looking round, Barbara realised that already uniforms were less prevalent.

"Lord Osborne! Could you escort myself and Miss Campion back to my house? The poor child feels faint."

The gentleman expressed himself delighted to be of service, and said that the heat, which had persisted despite every door and window being flung wide, was undoubtedly responsible for Miss Campion's indisposition.

"Once you're in the fresh air, you'll feel more the thing," he prophesied.

So soon enough Barbara found herself back in Alicia's bedchamber, tearing off her borrowed plumes and donning shirt and breeches once more.

"Fancy Captain Alleyn recognising you when

Harry did not!" Alicia marvelled, hanging the primrose gown back in her closet. "He danced with you,
too, and he scarcely ever dances. But you know that,
I suppose."

"No. Why not? Does he disapprove of dancing?"

"Gracious no, Babs! He's been wounded in the
right knee. It is healing well, I believe, but has been
very painful. I think he's afraid he might fall, or
stand on his partner's toes, or something. He's not
danced for over a year now."

"But he dances so well!" Barbara exclaimed,
removing her false ringlets with a regretful sigh.
"He's danced with me twice, and both times he
danced beautifully."

Alicia regarded her thoughtfully. "Yes. He likes
you, Babs, that'll be why. He must trust you not to
make a fool of him."

"Nonsense! He doesn't like me at all! The first
time he met me he flirted desperately and quite
frightened me by . . . well, quite frightened me.
Then when I joined the regiment and he found out I
was a girl, he was severe. He thinks I'm a fool to love
Harry, and Harry is a worse one to love me."

"If I were you, I'd ask myself if I really loved
Harry," Alicia said as they left the room and began to
descend the stairs. "Tell me more about this
arranged marriage of yours, Babs. I've had an idea."

"There isn't much to tell. Elmira explained that
old Lord Chacewater had been to the house and
asked for my hand in marriage. She says he's an old
friend of my father's and was asking me out of pity!
And then . . ."

"Wait a moment! *Elmira* told you? You never actually spoke to Lord Chacewater yourself? Nor even to your uncle?"

"Not a word," admitted Barbara. She opened the front door and peered cautiously out. "All's clear. I must be off, Allie; but a thousand thanks!"

"Wait a moment," Alicia said sharply. "Babs, if it was just Elmira's word, has it never occurred to you that she might be lying?"

"It might have, but Becky showed the gentleman in. And besides, what point would there be in lying on such a subject?" She ran down the steps and raised her hand in farewell. "Goodnight, my lady; and thank you!"

"Oh, but Babs, wait! There's something I don't believe you know! Do let me explain!"

"I can't wait, my lady; the Captain said twenty minutes. Goodnight."

Barbara melted into the shadows, leaving Alicia's voice fading into silence. It was dark, but she walked purposefully back towards the Rue de la Blanchisserie. Brussels was alive with soldiers and officers; voices called, feet tramped; their brigade was obviously not to be the last to set off for the battle front, then! She reached the Duchess of Richmond's house just as Daniel appeared in the doorway, glancing keenly round him.

He hailed her at once, in the businesslike tone she had come to expect when he addressed his stableboy.

"You're here. Good! My horse is being brought round, and . . . ah, here she is."

A lad scarcely larger than Barbara herself handed

Snowcloud's reins to the Captain, tugged his fore-
lock, and scampered off into the darkness, clutching
the largesse which Daniel had given him.

"Where's your horse, Bob? I take it you rode
in?"

"I let her loose in a field on the outskirts of the
city," Barbara admitted. "She's quite safe, and easy
to catch, but . . ."

"But not here when you need her. Never mind,
you'd best jump up behind me. I'll take you back to
the field with me. But I can't wait if Mollie refuses to
be caught quickly."

He mounted Snowcloud and Barbara, with a
desperate heave and a wriggle, got herself on to the
horse's snowy rump, saying breathlessly, "All right,
I'm aboard."

He chuckled, kicking the mare to a trot. "How
nautical. Better hang on, I'm in a hurry."

Barbara caught hold of his jacket – and very nearly
disappeared over Snowcloud's tail as the mare suddenly broke into a long, striding canter. Daniel called over his shoulder, "I said hang on!" and Barbara,
scowling, put both arms round his waist, telling
herself that in her role as stableboy it was the most
natural thing in the world to be riding pillion behind
Captain Alleyn with both arms round his waist, her
cheek pressed to the back of his jacket, and her heart
bumping wildly somewhere in the region of his
backbone.

Nevertheless, she was not sorry when the lights
grew farther apart and the houses began to be
replaced by hedges, and she was able to say breath-

lessly, "This next field, sir. If you could stop for a minute?"

He drew Snowcloud to a halt and before he could say a word she had slipped down and run into the field, grabbing the bridle which she had hung in the hedge.

"Moll!" The pony came eagerly out of the shadows, ears pricked, and took the apple she was offering. She slipped the bridle over the pony's ears, felt Mollie accept the bit and buckled it into place. Then she was up, her hands steady on the reins.

"All right?" Daniel, in the road, could see her only as a shadow, she realised.

"Yes, sir, I've mounted. You go on, Captain, and I'll shut the gate."

She strode through the gateway, caught the top bar of the gate with her foot as she passed it, tugged it until she felt it latch, then turned Mollie's head towards the farm.

CHAPTER
NINE

WHEN they reached the farm the company was forming up in the yard, for though it was still dark, on the eastern horizon a pale line of grey showed where the dawn would presently begin. Toby, in a state of great excitement, was running from horse to horse, checking that each had his bag of oats, his net of hay, and his full pack.

"Hi, Bob; see what you almost missed," he gasped, as Barbara flung herself off Mollie and ran into the stable for her own slender luggage. "Git Snowcloud's equipment out, will yer?"

Barbara rushed into the mare's stall, took down the haynet and the bag of oats and ran out again to hook them to Snowcloud's saddle.

"Sorry, Toby," she said breathlessly, as she ran to load up Mollie with her saddle and the rest of her paraphernalia. "I shouldn't have gone and left you with all this! What about Celt and Santander? Are they ready to leave?"

"Aye. We'll be a bit behind the column, though, because there's another spare prad. One of us'll lead two. Could you manage?"

"Of course. But why?"

" 'Cos Lieutenant Bloomin' Kimberley went and bought 'isself another prancer," Toby said bitterly. "Wot a thing to do, eh? Tisn't as if he's got a groom nor nuffin', only us. So we'll 'ave to take turns to lead two prads."

"What's the new horse like? What's it called?"

Toby snorted. "Robber Baron, would yer believe! A lummocking great black stallion, wiv a wicked eye and teef like tombstones."

Barbara sniggered. "Don't like him much, do you? Has he bitten you yet?"

"I'll darken 'is daylights for 'im if he tries," Toby said. "Orrible brute!" He added, with a reluctant grin as he caught Barbara's eye, "*Trod* on me, 'e did! Me, what's been brought up wiv 'osses! Crunch on me toes . . ." He sucked in his breath in remembered agony.

"Well, no wonder you don't like him," Barbara said. "I daresay you'd dislike any horse belonging to Harry, though. I'll lead it first go off."

"You can lead it second go off an' all," Toby said succinctly. "I'll tek Celt and Santander wiv pleasure."

Barbara raised her brows. "Bad as that, is he? Well, I don't mind. But can't we leave now? The column's almost out of sight."

"I'll bring Robber out to you then. I left 'im in the stable till the last minute, 'im being so nervy an' all."

Barbara sat Mollie patiently, and presently Toby reappeared with a rangy black stallion, whose rolling eyes and nervously skittering hooves did not augur well for their journey.

She took the lead rein, saying, "Where did Harry get him? He's nervous as a cat, not at all suitable for riding into battle, I should think."

"Ho, that isn't why 'is lordship bought 'im," Toby said scornfully. "He's got 'im for 'unting, if you please."

"Hunting?" Barbara said, considerably taken aback. "Well, I suppose Harry knows what he is doing." She dug her heels into Mollie and the pony moved forward. "Off we go. Can you manage Celt and Santander?"

"No bovver," Toby said. "You lead, Bob, and we'll foller. We'd best 'urry though, we don't want to get ourselves lost!"

"Lost? How could we?" Barbara said, twisting round in her saddle to stare at her companion. "We're going to the battle, we'll meet hundreds of troops bound in the same direction."

"Show's 'ow little you know," Toby said without rancour. "Battle fronts ain't that straightforward, bantling! They'll be spread over a couple of miles of country and more. But we'll be all right if we can catch up wi' the column."

Despite Barbara's forebodings, she soon began to enjoy her ride into the first faint light of dawn. The great expanse of sky over the flat country paled and paled until the stars were no longer visible and a faint line of rose-pink appeared on the horizon.

By the time it was full day, the countryside was strange to her, and the number of lanes and byways, all looking exactly the same, was causing confusion ahead. The column would halt, the men staring around them, whilst officers rode first along one branch of the track and then the other, trying to discover their way. In the end, Harry was sent to a small farmhouse and came back armed with directions which should lead them eventually to Braine le Compte.

But at last, ahead of them, they saw other columns of men and knew they had caught up with some of the army at least. They had been riding on a sort of plateau, but now they descended into marshy country and the narrow country lane along which they rode began, under the unaccustomed numbers and weight of the army, to deteriorate into a muddy morass which slowed them up considerably.

"It was pleasant on the plateau, but it's terribly hot down here," Barbara said, pushing the damp hair off her forehead. "Hello, what's holding us up ahead?"

It took them an hour to reach the obstruction and when Barbara saw it, she could not but feel concerned. A low and particularly marshy stretch of the road had been laid with long tree-trunks to form a corduroy road, but the road was little used, and the logs could not stand up to the sudden increase in traffic. By the time Toby, mounted on a pony but leading Celt and Santander, took his place to cross, the road resembled nothing so much as a bog littered with rotting tree-trunks.

Toby pressed forward and the pony and Santander managed to keep their footing but Celt, with a squeal of fear, sank up to his fetlocks in the rich mud.

"Bring the big 'un close to the 'edge," a Sergeant, standing on the far side of the boggy stretch, shouted. "It don't get no deeper, it's only because he's a powerful big prancer that 'e's sunk like that."

Taking his advice, Toby nudged Celt closer to the hedge and presently Barbara saw the three animals struggle on to firm ground once more.

"Come on now, lad," the Sergeant callèd, seeing Barbara apparently hesitating. "You saw the nipper 'ere come through it safe enough. Tek the plunge!"

"I'm *trying*," Barbara shouted back. "The pony'll go, but the stallion won't budge."

And indeed Robber, ears laid flat to his head, eyes bulging, made it perfectly clear that cross he would not.

"Try dismounting, and leading 'em both," the Sergeant suggested.

But nothing made the slightest difference. A column of infantry splashed stolidly through the bog, their officers riding beside them, but not even this example of British phlegm – for the soldiers were mired up to the knee – changed Robber's mind about the dangers of the road.

Barbara. driven to desperation, screamed to Toby, "Come back for Mollie, would you? I'm going to take him back, round to where the road's firmer and then put him to the bank. We'll ride across the marsh because that won't be poached by men and horses, and then I'll rejoin you the other side of the bog."

Toby obligingly came back for Mollie and then stood waiting on the far side of the corduroy stretch. "Just don't forget you've lef' me with four prads," he called gloomily as she turned Robber back the way they had come.

"I won't forget," Barbara said, giving a calculating glance at the height of the bank. She was so disgusted with her chicken-hearted mount that she had grave doubts of getting him to take the bank, but in this at least she wronged him, for having ascertained that it was a perfectly normal obstacle he pricked up his ears, snatched at the bit in a workman-like manner, and went over it like a cat.

Praising him lavishly, she then rode him across the marsh, keeping close by the bank until she saw Toby's spiky haircut protruding over the top of the grass. She went a little further, and presently was able to put Robber to a low place in the bank so that he slithered, muddy but safe, back on to the lane.

Toby, who had followed as well as he could with the other four horses, greeted her with undisguised relief. "We've lost the column well an' truly," he said. "Robber took the bank like a right 'un, though!"

"I suppose so," Barbara said, slipping off the tall horse and mounting Mollie, "but I'm sick and tired of him! If that's what Harry would call a proper high-bred 'un, then I'd rather have a sensible, sagacious animal like old Celt here. Look at him, mud up to his eyebrows and not so much as a buck or a rear when he slipped off those confounded logs!"

"You're fair covered wi' slush yourself," Toby remarked. "I say, Bob, what about suffin' to eat? I'm clemmed, I am!"

Barbara groaned. "We're ages behind the column! We might catch them up if we hurried on."

"I suppose you're right," Toby agreed.

They rode on, through the increasing heat of the summer day. Barbara shed her jacket, looping it through her stirrup leather. They crossed a stream and watered the horses, and Toby produced half a mud-splashed loaf and a chunk of cheese from his pony's haynet and eagerly divided the spoil. Barbara, with an equal lack of fastidiousness, ate her share with an excellent appetite, washing it down with a tin mug full of stream water.

"That *was* good," she said as, the last crumb eaten and the last drop of water drained, they remounted their ponies. "What's that noise ahead?"

Toby shrugged, but they found out soon enough. Further up the road, a troop of horse artillery were crossing the river Senne by a narrow stone bridge. Barbara and Toby watched as the great horses dragged the cannon up to the bridge and manoeuvred them across with skill and patience.

"Let's ask the officer where they're heading," Barbara said at last. It was easy to pick out the commanding officer, a harassed young man in his late twenties clad in a blue jacket faced with scarlet and gold, blue-grey breeches, and short boots. He had taken off his black bearskin helmet, which must have been unbearable in the heat, and was supervising the crossing of two hundred heavy horses, five nine-pounder cannons and the howitzer, as well as that of his junior officers and almost two hundred troopers.

He was still on their side of the river, fortunately, shouting instructions to "Keep the horses *together*, man! If they spread out they'll crush the gun carriage against the parapet."

Barbara waited for a pause in the proceedings and then said diffidently, "Excuse me, sir; could you tell me where you're heading? We've lost our company. It's Captain Alleyn's of the Rifle Brigade."

The Captain's attention did not stray from the last of the gun carriages, struggling over the narrow bridge, but he said, "The Rifles? No, I've seen no one and neither do I know where I'm heading. In fact, bantling, I'm just following the troops in front." The gun carriage lurched off the bridge on to the other side and the Captain turned to her for the first time, and grinned. "This whole business has been damnably mismanaged," he confided. "I had orders at first light to proceed to Enghien, where I would rendezvous with Major M'Donald. But damn me, if the Major was waiting for me there! So after lingering for almost an hour, we pressed on, as you can see."

"Then if we follow your guns, we shall arrive at the battle?"

"I hope so, yes."

A Sergeant on the opposite bank called across,

"Shall we move on, Captain Mercer, or shall we wait for the rest of the troop?"

"Move away from the river bank," roared Mercer. "We're almost over now; we'll join you presently." He turned back to Barbara. "I was saying you'll arrive at the battle, wasn't I? Well, I trust that's true, but I'm in a deuced pickle! My ammunition waggons were badly held up on a boggy strip of corduroy road, so I left them with my quartermaster-sergeant, Hall, in charge, thinking they'd catch us up. But they've not done so yet." He chuckled ruefully. "My first command, and I look likely to arrive on the field of battle with my guns and no spare ammunition! But I daresay they'll catch up with us before we go into action."

He nodded to them and went over to where a soldier stood, holding a big dapple-grey charger. Mounting, he urged the last men over and Barbara and Toby followed as close behind as they dared.

They continued to march in the rear of the artillery for the rest of the afternoon. They were in wooded country, which was cooler, but restricted their vision of the countryside about so that when they suddenly emerged above a little valley they pressed forward eagerly to see what lay ahead.

"See the smoke?" Toby said, gesturing. "And hear that noise?"

"Is it . . . cannon?"

"Aye. And the sharper sounds, like slaps, are muskets."

"Then that smoke over there is from the battle?"

"Aye. But it's a way off yet."

With that they began to descend the hill, and from the valley they could no longer see the smoke. But the gunfire came to them still, bringing its message of excitement, and fear.

CHAPTER
TEN

THEY spent the night in the little town of Nivelles, crammed into a hayloft with soldiers, servants and camp-followers. They knew that a battle had been fought at a place called Quatre Bras, and that the allies had been victorious, but very little more.

Despite their resolve to be up and away early, they both overslept and by the time they had begged some stale bread and a lump of evil, eye-watering cheese from the innkeeper whose loft had been given over to the army, they almost expected that battle would have been joined once more.

However, as they made their way up to where the battle had been, a surprise awaited them. They met the army, doggedly marching back on themselves. Barbara's heart lifted to see their own company and Toby, with a shout, rode his pony over to where Sergeant Tallow was marching, but she fell in beside Harry.

"Is it a retreat, then? I thought from what the soldiers were saying in Nivelles last night that we had won the day?"

"Yes, and so we did, for though we were heavily outnumbered, we held them off and held them off. And all the time we were being reinforced. In fact we were reinforcements ourselves, for we didn't arrive on the battlefield until the worst was over and the French had been driven out of the two farmhouses they'd taken earlier; Piraumont and Gemioncourt. I can tell you it was a bloody business! But damned exciting!"

"Then why are the army retr . . . I mean marching back the way they came?"

Daniel, who had been riding with the column, came up with them at that moment and said, "We weren't the only ones engaged yesterday. Marshal Blücher and his Prussians were terribly mauled at a place called Ligny. Their casualties were very heavy and they've had to retreat on Wavre, so we must go back too. You understand that, I'm sure. We're making for the village of Waterloo, but I doubt we shall get a billet. You'd best stay with the column until we see where we are to stand, and then you can take the spare horses to the rear."

He rode on past them. Barbara, having considered the matter, said, "Wavre and this . . . Waterloo . . . are in line with one another, I suppose? So even now the army under the Duke and the Prussian army under Marshal Blücher will be in line?"

"Aye, that's it," Harry said. "Wellington could not hold out at Quatre Bras knowing that the French could outflank him, could he? That could be damned unpleasant. And what's more, Colonel Alexander Gordon, who is one of the Duke's most trusted aides, says that Wellington had the Waterloo area surveyed and reconnoitred weeks since. He always fights best on ground of his own choosing."

"Yes. But I remember Mr. Symonds once telling me how awful a retreat was. Some people must be furious, I suppose."

"Oh, yes. No one likes to win and then abandon one's position. Picton's in a terrible rage over it. But the rumour goes that he was knocked down and may have broken some bones yesterday – enough to sour his temper, I suppose. How did you and Toby get on? You lost us, of course."

"Yes, thanks to your wretched Robber. He's no horse to campaign on, Harry!"

Harry grinned. "Nervy, ain't he? But what action! Smooth, tireless . . ."

"One glance at enemy troops and he'll carry you smoothly and tirelessly in the opposite direction," Barbara warned.

"Well, we've got 'em beat," Harry said light-heartedly. "Tomorrow, I suppose, the *coup de grâce* will be delivered, and then Robber will come into his own. I shall hunt him! Tell you what, Dabs, there's no reason for you to go to the rear; dull stuff! You stay nearby and watch the action! I say, was that rain?"

Barbara glanced up just as a tremendous peal of thunder seemed to split the sky, accompanied by flash after flash of lightning, and rain began to fall in torrents.

Robber, true to his reputation, reared and squealed and Barbara had her work cut out to hold him. She heard Harry shouting at her to go to the rear of the column but she had no choice but to remain where she was, falling into line behind

Harry, coaxing the horse forward as best she could.

Fortunately, being in column seemed to have a quieting effect on the stallion. He whinnied, but he stopped trying to break free, crowding so close to Mollie that Barbara's leg was in imminent danger of being flattened. She soothed him as best she could but otherwise she could do nothing, for the rain was so heavy that she could hardly make out the head and shoulders of Harry, riding in front of her.

It must have been nearly an hour later that the cloudburst gradually died away into more normal rain. Harry, glancing over his shoulder, said, "All right, Bob? I think we can't be far, now."

"I'm fine," Barbara said. "Soaked to the skin, but fine."

Daniel, riding up beside her, paused a moment to say briskly, "Wellington weather, you see, lad! All the Duke's successful battles are preceded by storms, so tomorrow will see us engaged to some purpose. You'd best find Toby and we'll see where you can best spend the night before going to the rear."

Barbara waited until he had ridden ahead and then pulled a face beneath her dripping shako. Retreat to the rear, indeed, with the baggage and the camp-followers! She smiled demurely, patting Mollie's soaking neck. *Just you try and make me, Captain Alleyn*, she thought. *Just try, that's all!*

"Very well, since it is late and the weather so foul, you'd best find what shelter you can, and sleep here. But tomorrow, at first light, you *must* withdraw.

Toby may stay with the spare horses, a little to the rear; we shall need them. But you, my child, must make your way back to Brussels. That's an order, Barbara."

Barbara and Daniel were standing in the drenching rain, talking in low tones. Glancing up at the face above her own, the firmness more marked than ever, the soaked wing of dark hair flattened above his bright, determined eyes, Barbara knew that he meant it.

"But I can't go to Brussels," she objected. "What on earth is the use of a spare pony, miles and *miles* behind the lines? You'll want every horse you can get here! And how will you explain to Toby that I'm being sent back, and the charge of all the horses is his alone? Especially Robber, who's so nervy and difficult."

"I'll send you with a message," Daniel said brusquely. "To Lady Birkenshaw. I'll explain and ask her to take care of you for . . . for Lieutenant Kimberley. Now you'd best make your way to wherever Toby is. The two of you will be safe enough. Lie on Toby's blanket and put yours over the pair of you."

"All right," Barbara said gloomily. Darkness had not much added to the doubtful charms of a soaked field of shoulder-high rye where every step taken meant sinking inches into the poached ground and dragging one's foot free with a gruesome sucking sound. And everywhere there were men, horses, baggage and equipment. All soaked, miserable, and, she imagined, apprehensively awaiting the morrow.

Looking around the crowded field, she wondered

wearily how long it would take her to find Toby, but she had barely walked more than a dozen yards when he hailed her. He was propped up under a hedge sheltered beneath a blanket.

"Hi, Bob, where you a'going? I've tied the prads to the 'edge. C'mon and get into what little shelter there is."

"Where's my blanket?" Barbara asked suspiciously, eyeing the sodden pile of baggage beside Toby.

"It's the one wot I've got draped over me," Toby said firmly. "Daubed wi' mud, it acts like a sorta tent, see?" He held out a fold. "Come on, git under."

Shivering, Barbara crawled into the slight shelter of the blanket, but though it was as clammy and unpleasant as might be supposed, it did seem to stop the rain actually cascading down upon them.

"What about food, Toby? I'm starved!"

"Commissariat's not reached 'ere yet," Toby said laconically. "So all you get is what you can find. Like some oats?"

He delved into his pocket and produced a handful of the horses' oats and Barbara took some and began to chew the kernels.

"To think I grumbled about that cheese," she groaned. "I wish we'd thought to bring some bread with us. Anything would be better than nothing. It seems *years* since I had a proper meal."

"Let's sleep, shall us?" Toby said. "No use whining for what we can't 'ave. I'll wake you if any food arrives."

But they were destined to get little sleep that

night. Time after time, horses broke loose from their tethers and galloped down the hill towards the château of Hougoumont. Every time, someone had to check that their own horses were safe, and after half-a-dozen false alarms it was discovered that Robber had really broken loose and careered down the hill with three or four other horses.

"We'd best go after 'im," Toby said wearily. In the darkness his face showed paper-white. "Else we might lose 'im."

"I'll go," Barbara said. "You went last time. You stay here."

She found herself glad enough to leave their cramped quarters and to stretch her legs a little. It was still raining, but wet as she still was from her previous soaking that, she felt, scarcely mattered at all. She looked round her in the dimness, saw one or two fires twinkling at intervals, and set off downhill,

She reached the huddle of outbuildings, but to cut Robber out from the herd was more than she had bargained for. Dim figures, an Ensign, a groom and an officer circled the beasts, trying to identify their own mounts but the horses, nervously shifting and pushing one another, proved impossible to catch.

The groom, a sturdy fellow with a sack over his head to protect him from the worst of the rain, said at last, "Leave be, fellows, leave be! They'll not go far till it's light, and we can come down 'ere first thing. I'm for getting some rest while we can."

The men drifted away and Barbara, after making one more abortive attempt to cut Robber out from the herd, decided to follow suit. Indeed, she thought yearningly, making her way up the hill once more, Toby's mud-daubed shelter seemed positively homelike when compared with the cold mud and the sharp wind and the continual downpour.

Slogging uphill with her head down, intent only on reaching shelter, Barbara ran straight into someone. There was a curse, hands flailed briefly, and then she and her assailant were struggling in the flattened rye.

"You want to look where you're going," the man began, and then exclaimed sharply and putting both hands beneath her armpits, hauled her to her feet. She began to apologise for bumping into him when he interrupted her, saying, "A woman, by all that's wonderful! Settlin' down as nice as you please in the rye, eh, my little pigeon?"

Barbara tried to pull herself free, saying in her gruffest voice, "You're mistaken, sir. I'm Bob Garland, of the Ninety-Fifth. Let me go at once!"

But the man had hold of her wrists and only laughed, clumsily prodding the front of her jacket with his free hand in a way which brought the blood rushing to her cheeks.

"Come wi' me, my pretty," he said in a thick voice. "I've got a neat shelter 'ere, but I was mortal cold! However, you'll soon warm me – and I you, gal!"

Barbara was in a dilemma. There were men bivouacking all around but if she managed to convince them she was a female in distress, her secret would be out. If she pretended to go willingly, she might yet escape and fly back to Toby. Down here

160

there was no shelter and no fires, either. Further up the hill she would be safe and he would never find her.

The man pulled her roughly over the muddied ground towards a gun carriage. Once there he fell to his knees, forcing her to do the same, and crawled under the canopy which formed a small, tent-like enclosure.

"What've you got there, Rigg?"

The sleepy voice, with its rich Irish accent, made Barbara's heart jerk with dismay. Another man shared the tent. Could she ever escape from two of them?

"A wench," Rigg said breathlessly. "Put another stick on the fire and I'll show ye."

Barbara, flat on her face in the mud, moved her head a little and saw a tiny fire and a huge, red-haired man, blanket draped, leaning against the gun carriage and eyeing her curiously.

"A wench? In breeches? Novu! Leave the lad go now, Rigg. You've mired him up to the . . . Oh!"

Rigg, jerking Barbara onto her knees, had torn her jacket open to show her shirt, wet and mudstained, moulded to her shape by the damp, and gaping open. She jerked forward, trying to hide herself, and saw her captor's mouth droop with lust and the other man's face redden.

"What did I tell ye, Seamus? Isn't she a lovely find for a wet, mis'rable night, eh? Look at those bubs! I've not 'ad a woman for longer than I care to think, but I'll 'ave one tonight or me name's not Jack Rigg!"

He pulled Barbara nearer him, then pushed her down on to the piece of canvas which was spread over the mud. She felt it sink slightly beneath her to take her weight, and then he was on her, one hand still holding her wrists captive, the other roving with hateful intimacy across her waist, feeling for the fastening of her breeches.

She gave a small, breathless scream and he laughed, then bent his head to kiss her. She gasped and kicked – then saw him suddenly recede from her. She rolled over, weeping jerkily, clutching at her shirt and jacket. She heard Seamus say soothingly, "Look, Rigg, I'll grant you t'ink she's a girl, but anyone who fights on this field wi' me is what they choose to be. See? Dis . . . dis young 'un's been to Quatre Bras, I'll warrant and she's . . . he's come here to fight. We don't want to stop the crature from doing his share tomorrow, do we? Might make the difference between life and deat' for one of us. Now leave the choild be!"

All the while he spoke he was holding the other man quite effortlessly, it seemed, with both arms twisted up behind his back.

Barbara, breathless and shaking with fright, backed towards the opening, fastening her jacket with fingers that trembled and shook.

"Now, Rigg, whilst you were out seeing after the hosses, didn't I manage to find a fat hen?" The Irishman's voice was gentle, persuasive. "A better bird you'll never find! And dere was I, only waitin' for you to come back before poppin' it into the pot . . ."

Barbara gabbled, "Thank you sir, thank you," and backed out of the tent.

The man called Seamus said cheerfully, "T'ink nothin' of it, just you skedaddle, now!" And then, to his companion, "No messin' now, Rigg me boyo, and sure an' I'll let you go. You pass over the pot an' I'll produce me bird!"

Barbara, trying her best to run uphill, glanced behind her, but realised there would be no pursuit. The Irishman, God bless him, had too strong a character for that. And too strong an arm as well! She was deathly tired, however, and covered in mud from head to toe. Toby would be none too pleased to see her so mired, but there was no help for it.

A voice from the hedge hailed her as she drew nearer to Toby's shelter.

"Bob! Over here!"

She glanced nervously towards the voice, to see two men crouched in the shelter of an enormous umbrella and warming themselves before a sizeable fire. One was the young artillery-captain who had been kind to her and Toby earlier in the day, and the other was Captain Alleyn.

"Yes, sir?" she said, approaching cautiously.

Captain Alleyn looked at her curiously. "What a state you're in, Bob! You've no clean clothes with you, I suppose? But they'd be soaking, in any case. Well, well. Come and have a warm."

Barbara went over and crouched by the fire, holding out her hands to the blaze. She was shivering uncontrollably and her wrists were bruised and scratched where Rigg had held her. She had mud all over her front and two buttons were missing from her jacket. Her shako had gone long since and her curls were plastered flat to her skull.

Captain Mercer said curiously, "What happened to you, boy? You're the lad I met yesterday, aren't you? What reduced you to this state?"

"The horses broke loose," Barbara said. "I followed them down to the château and I caught hold of the one I was looking after and slipped on the mud and was dragged. I didn't catch him, either."

The explanation seemed to satisfy both men, though Barbara thought Daniel looked at her a trifle thoughtfully. But all he said was, "Come under the umbrella, then you'll have a chance to dry out."

Unable to think of any good reason for disobeying and certainly not wanting to disobey, Barbara crept round beneath the umbrella and sat on the slight bank of the hedge as the two men were doing. They began to chat quietly; of the battle at Quatre Bras, of the battle that was to come. Once, she heard Daniel ask Captain Mercer – who turned out to have the unusual name of Cavalié – "Why the umbrella?"

The artilleryman chuckled. "My second Captain always carries it. But he's managed to find himself a billet, so he lent it to me. We laughed at him on the march, I can tell you! My command is 'G' Troop of the Horse Artillery and we were chosen to remain in the rear with the cavalry to cover the retreat. We did so, but of course it meant that we were literally chased by the French. And then, of course, the storm broke. Well, there we were, flying for our lives, with Lord Uxbridge galloping alongside us crying, 'Make haste! For God's sake, gallop, or you will be taken!' It is no easy thing, sir, to gallop those great heavy horses of ours when they're dragging the gun carriages, but gallop we did. Imagine, the cloudburst, the French chasseurs following us through some little village – and my second captain, galloping with the best, with that wretched umbrella up to protect him from the downpour!''

"What a marvellous picture!" Daniel said. "How the French must have laughed! But tell me, did they use Whinyates' rockets? I heard that the Duke forbade him to bring them, and then relented. Were they used?''

"They fired them," Captain Mercer admitted. "They aimed them at the French, of course, but I agree with the Duke that they're dangerous! The first one streaked at a gun emplacement and exploded, and all the French promptly deserted their posts, even those troopers manning neighbouring guns. But the other rockets! Some went straight up in the air, but one turned round and chased me! A great fool I must have looked, turning and doubling up the road with one of Whinyates' rockets close on my tail! But it came nearer killing me than any French chasseur!''

Daniel laughed. "There's always one damned funny incident in every battle, and you've already provided me with two! Now, as to tomorrow . . . .''

The talk grew technical, the fire warmed her clothes to a gentle steam, and Barbara became very comfortable and very, very drowsy. She knew she was slowly sliding sideways but was incapable of stopping herself. And anyway, she soon found herself nestling against something warm and comforting.

She slept, sinking fathoms deep into slumber.

CHAPTER
ELEVEN

BARBARA awoke to find herself curled within the shelter of a protective arm, as warm and comfortable as if she had been in her own bed. She moved, muttering, unable to remember, for a moment, where she was or who held her so close.

Then a voice, loud and accusing, said, "Babs!"

She stirred again as another voice said softly, "Hush, man. Let her wake soft, she had a difficult night of it."

Her eyelids flew open and she struggled into a sitting position, to find herself looking up into Captain Alleyn's face. He smiled at her, the look in his eyes disturbingly intimate.

"Good morning, Bob. You slept like a log, my child!"

Harry, standing a few feet in front of her, said furiously, "My God! Why, you . . . he . . ."

Barbara, blushing hotly, scrambled to her feet. A quick glance told her that both Captain Cavalié Mercer and his big umbrella had gone. "I'll go and get Robber back," she said. "I know where he is, Lieutenant Kimberley. It was trying to get him back for you in the night that led to my being dragged in the mud, and losing Toby, and . . ."

"Oh yes? I'll hear a round tale, if you please! And why Robber should be blamed . . ."

Daniel, getting to his feet, said quickly, "All right, Harry, the night's over, the rain has stopped, and we've a battle to fight today. Let's begin as we mean to go on, eh? How did you spend the night?"

"Not in a woman's arms," Harry said hotly, and Barbara saw the smile wiped from Daniel's face.

"Mind your tongue," he said. "The child was soaked and chilled to the bone. You settled yourself snugly somewhere, without a thought for her. Did you expect me to let her die of exposure?"

Harry, blushing, stuttered, "Y-you had n-no right to . . . to cuddle Babs like that! I c-can tell you, this p-puts a different complexion . . ."

"I'd better go and get Robber," Barbara said. "Has the commissariat come up yet? I'm starving!"

She turned on her heel and began to jog down towards the château, but Harry hurried after her, catching her arm and dragging her to a halt.

"Well, Babs? I find the girl I want to marry, who is almost my affianced wife, in the arms of another man . . ."

"Don't be so *silly*," Barbara cried, stung. "I fell asleep and sort of sagged against Captain Alleyn, that's all! He was snugly situated under the hedge with Captain Cavalié Mercer of the Horse Artillery. They had a lovely fire, and a great big umbrella. Why, I might easily have fallen against Captain Mercer, I suppose! Oh, Harry, I was so *cold*, and I'd been knocked down by the horses, and . . ."

"You'll have to find a better excuse than that

before I offer you marriage," Harry said furiously.
"If you wanted to be cuddled . . ."

"I did *not* want to be cuddled!" Barbara shrieked,
glaring at him. "Leave me alone, Harry! And I don't
want to marry you! You're quite the nastiest, most
suspicious, evil-minded young man I've ever met!
Now go away and let me get on with my job!"

"How dare you call me names! How dare you . . ."

Barbara gave Harry a long, contemptuous glance
and turned away, leaving him standing in the mud
with his mouth open, then ran down towards the
group of dejected horses still standing uncertainly
against the château wall.

She returned to find a chattering group round a
fire, on which steamed a cauldron of something
which smelled appetisingly like breakfast.

"Hi, Bob, there's a stirabout," Toby called as she
approached. "And 'ot, sweet tea!"

Taking the plate which he handed her, Barbara
began to tuck into the porridge but said to Harry,
between mouthfuls, "So the commissariat did catch
us up!"

It was meant to be conciliatory, but he turned his
shoulder on her, so she addressed herself to Daniel.
"Well sir, it is morning. What must Toby and I
do?"

"You must make your way to the rear, we'll be
taking up positions soon. But I want you to ride into
Brussels, both of you, at the least sign of danger,
taking the spare horses with you. I'll accompany you
to a place of safety myself," he turned to Harry.
"Unless you will deputise for me, Harry?"

It was an olive branch, but Harry said stiffly, "No, thanks. You'll see them safe, I'm sure."

Presently, breakfast finished, the spare horses rounded up, Barbara mounted Mollie. She could hear the crack of gunfire clearly and every now and then the wind would bring a mutter of French from the enemy lines. Leaning down from the pony's back, she put a tentative hand on Harry's arm.

"We're off now, Harry. Take care!"

He would not unbend, however, merely giving her an indifferent glance and saying, "Off, are you? No doubt we'll meet after the battle."

Barbara swallowed. "Harry, I'm sorry . . ."

He turned from her, calling, "George, do you ride Hannibal or Celt this morning?"

Daniel, at Barbara's elbow, said softly, "Don't fret, child, he'll come round. His pride's been hurt. Now we really must leave."

With Toby and the spare horses, they made their way into the small village scarcely more than half a mile from where battle fronts were forming.

"Mont St. Jean," Daniel said. "The horses will be safe enough here, unless the battle moves this way. At the first sign of such troop movements, you two will make for Brussels. Do you hear me?"

"Yes, sir," Toby said, and winked at Barbara.

"You, Bob, come with me. I want a quiet word with you."

He led her a little apart, until they were out of Toby's hearing. "This is *the* battle, Barbara, and I think we all know it, veterans and Johnny Raws alike. Did you see the French massing?"

Barbara shook her head.

"It was an awesome sight. The *colours*, Barbara! The chasseurs in brilliant green and purple, yellow and scarlet, the hussars in blue and red, dragoons with tiger-skin helmets, the cuirassiers' helmets crested with copper and floating horsehair, and the the carabiniers, all over six foot in height and wearing white, with breastplates of gold and red corded helmets. The glinting of metal, the glowing coats of the horses, all spread out in the soft sunrise. Yes, an awesome sight. And most of them are hardened veterans. We've got more than our share of youngsters who've never fired a gun in anger, and foreigners who don't know the Duke well enough to trust him.

"Oh, we're going to *win*," he added, seeing Barbara's eyes widen. "Don't worry about that! But it'll be a close thing. A lot depends on whether the Dutch and Belgians stand; the Duke has always feared they might suddenly go over to the enemy, you know. And more, perhaps, on whether the Prussians man age to come up. Blücher, grand old boy that he is, says he'll bring his troops up somehow, but it'll be close if he can't manage it." He looked down at her, his expression at once tender and serious. "I . . . I cannot tell what changes may take place, in the course of today. I have written out a letter three times, and given one copy to George, one to Harry, and I have the last one here, for you. If I'm . . . unable to assist you myself, I want you to go straight to Lady Birkenshaw and tell her who you are; who you *really* are, Barbara. And then give her the letter."

He handed her an envelope and Barbara, after a cursory glance, slid it into her pocket.

"I'll go to Lady Birkenshaw if you and Harry and George are all . . . all killed," she stammered. "But why? And why three copies of the letter?"

"It's my will, among other things," Daniel said curtly. "You, my child, are vulnerable also, don't forget! If you are killed, then perhaps one of the others will get through."

"Oh!" Barbara said, digesting this. "I thought the letter explained my presence to her ladyship."

"It does, as well as other things. But let be! I hope I'll be taking it from you and introducing you to her ladyship myself this evening. Or Harry will."

Barbara stared at him. "H-Harry? Oh, but . . ."

She wanted to tell him that Harry mattered not one jot. She wanted to cry, *It's you, Daniel, you! It is you who must not be hurt!*

But he was saying gently, "You're upset by Harry's attitude; don't be! He's jealous! When this is over he'll want to marry you as much as you want to marry him! And once you're betrothed he won't be jealous of every man who smiles at you."

He patted her shoulder, then mounted Snow-cloud.

"Take care of each other," he called over his shoulder as he cantered back the way they had come.

Barbara rejoined Toby. Harry would want to marry her as much as she wanted to marry him? Then he would not want to marry her at all! And Daniel? How did he feel?

"Come on, Bob," Toby said impatiently. "Don't

dream! Let's get the prads quartered at this 'ere big farm, shall us?"

The farm was deserted except for the fat and jolly farmer's wife, who told them they might stable the horses and welcome. She told them to help themselves to fruit and vegetables, gave them a drink of milk, and then pottered back into her large farm kitchen to boil mash for the hens.

When the horses were settled, Toby and Barbara climbed up to the hayloft, from which vantage point they could see right up the road leading to and from the battlefield, and hear the mutter of cannon, the sharp smacking reports of muskets, and the buzzing whine of grape and cannister-shot – assorted delicacies, the troops called it, with mordant humour.

"If we'd been nearer, we'd have 'eard the song the French always sing when a battle's about to commence," Toby said with gory relish. "They say it's the last sound many a soldier hears." He grinned at Barbara's anxious face and sang, in his execrable French,

> *"L'Empereur recompensera,*
> *Celui qui s'avancera!"*

"And I know what it means, too, Bob! The Emperor pays soldiers who advance!"

"More or less," Barbara admitted. "What's that?"

"Which? I can 'ear bells, and . . . that thundering noise? That's a cavalry charge."

Barbara shuddered. "Then I suppose it's really started?"

Soon enough, they had proof, had it been needed. Wounded men began to trickle down the road towards Mont St. Jean.

"I'll nip down and see if there's news," Toby said.

"I'll come too," Barbara said. "What was *that*?"

In front of their very eyes a waggon, trundling down the road, had disappeared in a great cloud of noise and smoke.

"Shell," Toby answered laconically. "They're not shelling us, some gunner's got 'is range wrong, that's all. Still want to come down?"

"Yes," Barbara said firmly, and together they went down into the farmyard.

For hours, the wounded continued to come. Bullets flew round the rooftops, shells whistled overhead or crashed into trees and cottages. But the men continued to make their way into the courtyard, then into the farm or outbuildings. Barbara and Toby dispensed water, makeshift bandages, and what comfort they could.

"Are the sweeps engaged? Course they are! Everyone's engaged this time," a young Lieutenant whose arm had been blown off at the elbow told them whilst they bandaged the stump with what skill they could. "But I'm glad I lived to see the charge of the heavy cavalry. By God, what a sight! Nothing could withstand 'em! The Union and Household Brigades it was, and they swept across country with a thunder like that storm a night or so back, and smashed up against the French Cuirassiers, then through them, the horses fighting as well as the men! Their Colonel had both his arms shot off, but he gripped the bridle between his teeth and charged forward, shrieking to his men to follow."

"What 'appened?" breathed Toby. He had known war all his little life, but this was a battle like none which had gone before.

"They smashed the French infantry, but they went too far. It was a kind of divine madness. They struck through the French ranks with the power and speed of their thrust, but went on, and the ranks closed behind them. A handful came back, only a handful."

"And the Rifles?" Barbara said with painful eagerness. "We've . . . we've not seen any of our brigade amongst the wounded."

"They'll be well to the fore," the man said wearily. "They won't send their wounded back through the lines. They'll put them in the centre of the square, and close up. That's the way they fight."

Barbara felt the blood drain from her face but she finished her bandaging and patted the man's shoulder. "There's a surgeon coming round soon; he'll do what he can for you."

She moved on to the next man.

"They hammer and hammer and we stand, stand, stand," groaned a young trooper. "Sir Thomas Picton's dead, but still we stood. They charged the squares, and we piled the dead in the centre and closed ranks. They say the Twenty-Seventh Regiment died to a man, still in square." He looked up at Barbara and grinned suddenly, teeth white in his muddied, dirty face. "But we'll win, Miss! We will! I can tell, I have this . . ."

Before her eyes his young face stiffened, his grey eyes glazed, and he fell back on the hay.

Barbara, crying soundlessly, wondered, as she propped the veteran next to him up so that he could drink, why the boy had known her for a young woman. Had the closeness of his impending death opened, before closing for ever, his eyes?

But there was no time for conjecture, no time for mourning. She moved on to the next man.

"The Prussians arrived! We've not given an inch, despite the pounding we've taken. But it's a wonder to me there are any left alive. *Some* ran, but only foreigners and children. A Dutch-Belgian regiment and some of the Hanoverian Hussars left the field, but the Hussars were toy soldiers, who'd never been meant to fight. And the *real* Hanoverians – God, how they fought. There's a farmhouse which both sides wanted, La Haye Sainte. The Hanoverians held it and held it. It was fired twice, to my knowledge. They say the wounded roasted to death in the haylofts before the French broke in. They'd run out of ammunition by then, the Hanoverians, and they fought on still, with their hands and their bayonets. But we're safe now. The Duke has given the order to advance! You could hear the cheer in Brussels, I should think. Just after that I got mine."

He indicated his wounds. He was a young red-haired man, his face a mass of freckles, his eyes bright. From a Highland regiment, he wore the kilt and Barbara, looking compassionately down at him, could imagine the swagger with which he would walk. Would have walked. The surgeons were going to amputate his right leg at the knee, and probably his right hand. But the indomitable cockiness, the life surge in him, would not be damped. He was on fire with excitement, longing to know what was happening on the battlefield, supremely indifferent to his own fate.

"What next?" Toby asked.

The young Scot's eyes shone. "Why, victory, boy, victory! We're advancing, chasing them back where they belong, into France. The Duke was everywhere, and he knew when the moment came. 'Damn it,' he shouted, 'in for a penny, in for a pound!' And then he took off his hat and waved it in the air three times. How they cheered! And by God, how they charged!"

It was dark before they knew for certain it was over. Even then, rumours persisted. But by half-past ten, with the moon up, Barbara told Toby she must find out what had happened.

"I'm going back," she said. "If it's all over, why haven't they returned? None of them!"

"They're chasing Boney back into France," Toby said. His faith in his companions was absolute; they could not let him down by getting killed, he was sure of it.

"But what if some of them are wounded?"

Toby sighed. "I'll come with you."

They passed out of the courtyard and on to the

road. The fresh, chill night air was sweet in their nostrils after a day spent tending the sick and the dying. But all along the road, grim reminders of the battle met their eyes. Dead bodies, fallen by the roadside on their way to the dressing stations, and horses, mortally wounded, horrified Barbara so much that she walked stiffly, eyes only on the road at her feet.

In twenty minutes they had arrived at their destination. Here, the fields were sown with the wounded, the dead, the dying. It was impossible to tell friend from foe, the living were encamped amongst the dead, too worn out to move, bivouacking where they stood.

Toby clutched Barbara's arm. "Let's go back," he muttered, and she felt him shake. "I – I don't care for nuffin', you know that, but I can't face this. One of them bodies could stretch out a 'and, or a knife, and . . ."

"But the *Company*," Barbara said. She was so afraid that her teeth were chattering, but she felt that search she must.

"We'll never find 'em," Toby pleaded. "Not in this damned, tricksy moonlight. We'll come again, at first light!"

"But what if they're wounded," began Barbara, her voice breaking. For the wounded lay everywhere, unheeded. Men groaned for water in more tongues than she had known existed. She could see them on either side of her, but knew she could walk past her dearest friends in this light without recognising them.

"Come on, Bob," urged Toby. He had hold of her hand and at last, reluctantly, she turned with him.

She was sobbing beneath her breath, bitterly tired, filled with horror at the sights around her, swamped with sadness that it should have come to this. The hopeful faces, the brilliant uniforms, the pride, lying broken and dying in the mud of the victorious battlefield.

Without another word they made their way, hand in hand, back to Mont St. Jean.

CHAPTER
TWELVE

THEY slept by the roadside in the end, curled up like a pair of puppies, grateful for each other's warmth. They could not return to the farm, for every available space was packed with wounded, and in their exhaustion, indeed, the grassy verge was a comfortable bed.

The sun woke them.

Toby sat up, knuckling his eyes. "Another 'ot day," he said. "Shall us 'ave breakfast?"

Barbara, sitting up too, merely shook her head.

"Oh! Well, chances are there's nuffin' for the likes of us, anyroad." He got to his feet, yawning and stretching. "Back up there, is it?"

"We must!" Barbara said desperately.

They'd not gone more than a few yards, however, when the first of the wounded, supporting a companion, came up the road towards them.

"One of ours!" Toby exclaimed, seeing the stained green jacket. "Oh, Mr. Wallace, 'ow are you?"

Rifleman Wallace's broad grin was good to see. "Not so bad, Toby. But poor Billing's not too good. Will you give me a 'and wiv 'im, back to the surgeon?"

Toby nodded. " 'Course. You go on, Bob, and I'll catch you up later."

Barbara continued up the road. She passed sights so terrible that she knew her mind would never be free of them. The dead, she began to think, were the lucky ones. And then, coming down the road towards her, came a man leading a horse, lame in its off-fore. It was Harry.

He saw her as she began to run and they met in the middle of the road in a hard embrace, with Barbara, almost crying with joy, stammering out her questions.

"You're alive! Oh, thank God! And Captain Alleyn? George? Oh, Harry, I've been so worried!"

"Yes, I'm alive and unhurt. Poor Pryall's dead, and Crimmond, Eeles, that old devil Radford; Babs, there has never been a battle like it! Everyone says so! The Duke *cried*, Babs, when he looked round the field. You've no idea . . . nor should you have! Oh, dear little Babs, I've come to take you back to Brussels. We'll get married, and we'll be happy, I swear it. It's Dan I've got to thank, you know. He sent me ahead of the brigade, and told me to take you to Lady Birkenshaw and she'll make all tidy."

Barbara gently put his arms away from her. "Is Daniel all right?"

"He's all right, but Snowcloud was killed. Poor Taffy was shot under me, a cannonball blew his hindquarters right off, he died instantly, thank God. It would have been a hard thing to shoot such an old friend. And George lost Hannibal and Celt. It's been . . . I can't describe it!"

"I know. Toby and I went up to the battlefield to try to find you last night."

"My poor girl! We slept where we stood. Robber was wounded in the off-fore, as you can see, and he lay down and I against him. I thought I'd never sleep, with the groaning for water all around. Yet I did."

He put his arm round her, turning her gently to face, not the battlefield, but back towards Mont St. Jean.

"No, I must go to the battlefield," Barbara said.

"I suppose you want to thank Dan," Harry said indulgently, "but you must come to Brussels with me. Don't you see, if we slip back there now, with all this excitement going on, you may take your place at Lady Birkenshaw's without any fuss? Dan thought of everything. He told me what to do this morning, while we were getting the company together."

Barbara took an undecided pace back towards Brussels.

Coming up the road towards them was a peasant, leading two Percheron horses. Barbara's mind registered that one horse pulled a cart and that the other was sound in wind and limb and held only by a rope.

"Of course, Dan's accustomed to thinking for others," Harry was saying. "His father, the Earl of Chacewater, wanted to have him out of the army, because his elder brother has been none too stout and then . . ."

Barbara stopped short. "The Earl of Chacewater? Captain Alleyn's *father*?"

"Yes. Didn't you know?"

"Then why is the Earl of Chacewater dangling after a wife?"

"Rubbish, Babs, what a tarradiddle! He's been a widower twenty years! What gossip is this?"

Barbara was eyeing the rapidly approaching horses. "Was there talk, gossip, perhaps, of *Dan* – I mean Captain Alleyn – making a female an offer before he left for Belgium?"

"He did propose to some chit," Harry admitted. "We pulled his leg about it, for it was some little wench he met in our part of the world, at a dance. Thought a lot of her, though he only met her the once. Love at first sight, eh? His father was to have sent him an express with the girl's answer, but it's not come yet. She'll be glad to have him when she hears he's a hero of . . . well, whatever this battle will be called. The Prussians want to call it La Belle Alliance, after the inn where Napoleon spent the night, but Dan reckons the Duke will call it Waterloo, because that's where *he* spent the night before the battle, and that's how his battles are always named. Babs! What. . . ?"

But Barbara was scrambling up on to the Percheron's broad, dappled back. Snatching the rope out of the startled peasant's hand she said apologetically, "It wouldn't have worked, Harry. I couldn't go back to Brussels and marry you! I've got to see *him*!"

With that she dug her heels into the Percheron's barrel sides and hit him across the neck.

"Giddup!" she commanded sharply, and then, as he began to lumber forward, she leaned along his neck and fairly shrieked into his cocked grey ear.

A shudder of surprise ran along the broad back, and then the Percheron leapt forward and went tearing down the road at a rolling gallop, leaving Harry standing, mouth agape, looking after her.

"So it was Dan!" he muttered. "It was Dan all along!"

He stood in the middle of the road for a moment, absently patting Robber's shoulder. Then he set off towards Mont St. Jean once more.

The battlefield was quieter now. Many had died in the night, others had been succoured by their companions. Barbara could see peasants moving slowly amongst the bodies, looting.

Ahead of her, she saw a man in rifle green tending another. She steered her mount towards them.

"Sergeant Tallow!"

The Sergeant got to his feet and grinned, pushing back his shako and blinking in the bright sunlight. "Bob! Good to see you, lad. This 'ere's Lieutenant Farrier, one of ours; he's wounded in the lungs and needs a doctor. Could you take 'im back to the dressing station for me?"

"Could you take him?" Barbara said, slipping down from the horse. "I've got to find the other officers."

"I don't want to leave the wounded. I've still got a musket that works, and . . ."

"I could wait here until you return," Barbara offered.

Sergeant Tallow shook his head. "It's the peasants, lad. They'd not be put off by a stripling. They rob the dead and kill the living, in their greed. I'm standing guard."

"I see," Barbara said, her stomach turning. "Then I'd better . . ."

But at that moment a burial party came marching over the field towards them and the peasants, staggering under their loads, began to shamble in the opposite direction.

"There, that's lucky," Sergeant Tallow said. "If you're sure you want to press on and don't need the 'orse, I'll take the Lieutenant up before me. You'll find the company further up the road; they joined in the pursuit, you know. I think they're searching the wood ahead for wounded."

Barbara helped him to lift the unconscious officer on to the Percheron's back and then began to trot up the road until she entered the shelter of the wood. She had barely been walking for five minutes before she heard voices and into view marched a weary column of men in rifle green. It was "D" company, but Daniel was not among them.

"I've a message for the Captain," she said, as the leading man hailed her. "Where is he, please?"

"The Captain? He's taken his canteen to refill. There's a stream a bit into the wood," a rifleman volunteered. "We're to march on to Mont St. Jean, where he will catch us up."

"Thanks, I'll find him," Barbara said.

She watched the company until it disappeared round the corner, then plunged into the wood.

It was almost pleasant in the wood with the sun-

shine falling, dappled, through the branches overhead. Birds sang, but otherwise it was quiet; too
quiet. No noise of small animals, no noise of men. As
she pressed forward, she saw why the little animals
had taken refuge elsewhere. On the soft moss,
cushioned by beech mast, they lay; the quiet and
innocent dead. Many were French, she could tell by
their uniforms; a cuirassier still in his heavy, glinting
armour, a French hussar with a face as beautiful and
untouched as a girl's, a member of the Imperial
Guard, a giant of a man in his blue campaigning dress
with the great bearskin helmet still on his head, and
his parade uniform spilling out of the knapsack on
his shoulders.

There were no wounded left here to groan out
their pain; the Company had done their work well.
And presently, as she walked, she heard the liquid
tinkle of a stream, and knew she was nearing her
destination.

She emerged from the trees on to the bank, and
saw him.

He had stripped off his jacket and shirt and was,
wincingly, mopping at an ugly furrow ploughed
across his side. From where she stood she could see
that the ball had passed beneath his arm, channelling
its way through his flesh as it went. It was, she knew,
only a deep graze, yet she felt her stomach contract
with sickness for his pain.

She heard her own voice say, "Captain Alleyn?"
but he gave no indication that he heard and she
realised that he was deaf; deafened by the noise of the
guns, as he was grimed by their smoke.

She moved forward like a sleepwalker, intent only upon being near him, not planning her next move, her next words even. She said, "Daniel?" and either a sound or a movement caught his attention for he glanced towards her, the blood-stained rag stilled, his face, now that she could see it full on, grimed and weary beyond description.

"Daniel, I . . . Harry came for me, but I . . ."

She was within two feet of him, suddenly desperately uncertain, trying to find an explanation for her presence. But it was not needed. He threw down the piece of rag, took a step towards her, and gathered her into his arms as a starving man might reach for food.

"My darling! My little darling!"

His clasp tightened as Barbara held up her lips to him, clinging like a burr, her arms round his naked neck, seeking for words to tell of her love. But she knew, as his kiss warmed and deepened, as her fluttering heart and body were crushed close, that words were not necessary. She was telling him she loved him as her mouth softened beneath his, as her body melted closer to him.

Presently he held her away from him, smiling down at her.

"How long have you known it was me?"

"From that first dance, on the terrace," she muttered. "Except that I didn't know what it *was* that I felt." She looked down at the wound in his side, oozing blood. "Daniel, let me fasten a pad over your wound, or you'll be ill, and unable to marry me tomorrow!"

He held her lightly by the hips, swaying her body gently, his eyes tender on her face. "Marry you? Who mentioned marriage?"

"You shocking rake! How can you cuddle me, and you half-naked, and *not* marry me? Besides, you have offered for me, haven't you?"

He grinned ruefully, struggling into his shirt whilst she held the pad in place over his wound. "Harry told you? Curses, now I shall have to do the right thing by you!"

He fastened his shirt, then began to struggle into his jacket.

"How nearly, how *very* nearly, you were killed," she said, seeing the pad over the wound within inches of his heart. "I would have died too, Daniel. I thank God that you were spared."

Her voice was trembling and he took her in his arms again, gently kissing her eyelids, her wet cheeks, then her soft mouth.

"Sweetheart, it's over, and we're both safe. I'll take you back to Brussels, and we'll marry as soon as may be. And we'll be together then, whether it's with the army or back on my father's estate. Now let me see you smile!"

Mistily, she smiled up at him. "Oh Daniel, I do love you!"

"And I you. One more kiss, and then we had best make our way back to Mont St. Jean, and the brigade."

They were back on the road before she spoke again.

Stopping dead in the middle of the carriageway,

she said, "Daniel, I'm still in boy's clothes! What will everyone think?"

He laughed, putting his arm round her waist. "I can't imagine! But they won't need to wonder for long; we'll have a military marriage, and you'll be a soldier's wife. I'm afraid your campaigning days are by no means over, love, for I shall want to see this whole mess cleared up before I sell out."

"I don't care," she said. "Oh, Daniel, whatever will we say to Toby? It *is* going to be difficult."

"It won't be easy," he agreed. "Are you sure you want to go through with it? If you'd prefer it, I could take you back to Lady Birkenshaw and marry you quietly, in a few months, when the regiment will be returning to England."

She smiled up at him suddenly, all doubts and difficulties set at rest. "And be without you, when I could be close to you? We'll marry at once, do you hear? I'll face Toby, and George, and Sergeant Tallow, everyone, sooner than be parted again. With you beside me, I'm prepared to follow the drum for the rest of my life!"

Arms round each other, they began to walk back towards Mont St. Jean.